I0630558

SIMON ORÉ MOLINA

S N A P !
C R A C K L E !
F U C K
Y O U !

ERASERHEAD PRESS

PORTLAND, OREGON

ERASERHEAD PRESS
833 SE Main Street #342
Portland, OR 97214

www.eraserheadpress.com
facebook/eraserheadpress

ISBN: 978-1-62105-282-1
Copyright © 2021 by Simon Oré Molina
Cover copyright © 2021 Steven Chunn

Printed in the USA.

SIMON ORÉ MOLINA

SNAP!
CRACKLE!
FUCK
YOU!

a cerealand mystery

To the Kellogg brothers.

PART ONE
GREEN CLOVERS

This story isn't really a story; it doesn't have a satisfying conclusion or a happy ending, it's not going to be that amusing to read. I am not sure myself how the story goes yet, I'm still living it, but I know it's not going to be good—because it's *my* story. I am twenty-nine years old, and I have been working in a cereal themed "amusement park" for almost ten years. I have put amusement park in quotes because I need everyone to understand that this is less of a park and more like the worst (or best, depending on who you are) parts of Amsterdam masquerading as a cereal themed theme park. Living in Cerealand is a fucking nightmare. It takes all my strength every day not to slit my throat and let the blood rain out onto the crunchberry tree outside my workstation. I'm sure you'd say "Why don't you just quit, if you hate it so much?"—but obviously, you don't understand anything. And fuck you.

I am standing on a hill above Marshmallow Meadow, and from the hill I can see most of the south side of the park—there are a few people on the Cocoa-

Coaster, but all in all, it's pretty dead for a Friday night. I light up a smoke, it's stale and it's a clove. Which I hate. But it's the only ones they let me smoke. I look at my pocket watch, she is very late.

I am waiting for Sam by the cinnamon tree like her note asked me to. I decide I will wait for another ten minutes. It is possible that her show ran long, the Toucan Sam show is still one of the more popular ones, even though Sam is not as young as some of the newest mascots. But even if she had a mirror or humiliation show afterward she should have been done by now. I hadn't heard from her in years, even though we both worked in the park I hardly saw her anymore. But the woman was wise to me, she knew that even after everything we'd done to each other, I would still show up.

Sam had insisted on meeting here after work. It wasn't like her to be so insistent on something but she had been very clear in her note that we were to meet here at 5 pm. I take out my watch again. It's almost 8. I hate myself for waiting this long. I feel stupid. I take one more look around, sure that Sam is about to show up, running up the hill, apologizing for losing track of time.

But she doesn't, so I go home.

I have to walk through the amusement park in order to get back to the dormitories. The park is closing for the night and it is dark and close to quiet—it's the only time I like this place anymore. The sky is a deep purple shade of blue and moonless with hardly any stars. It has been a few weeks since the moon has come out. Which is weird, I guess.

I walk by a few drunken park goers, stumbling to the exits, eating Cinnamon Toast Churros.

"Hey Lucky!" one of them yells out, "I'm gonna get yer lucky charms."

He throws his churro at me, it makes his drunk girlfriend laugh. The churro flies over my head, but almost knocks over my hat. The urge to do something, to break a bottle across both their faces for example, takes over me, and is strong. There are empty glass bottles all over the place, it would be pretty easy to do. The look of shock that I imagine they would make gives me a smile, but I let it go. I keep walking. Getting into fights, although totally allowed at the park, is a stupid idea. Even though I have been a leprechaun for over five years now I keep forgetting how small I am, how easy it would be for someone to kick me clear across a room like an empty box.

I started working at Cerealand about nine years ago. As a marshmallow sorter. Back then I loved cereal and the idea of a cereal themed amusement park seemed like a paradise. But the park wasn't for kids, so I wasn't even allowed to go until after I turned twenty-one.

Cereal wasn't really something that was marketed to kids anymore, it was more of a nostalgia product for adults. Most kids my age didn't like sweets and candy. Most of the kids I went to school with were either vegetarian or vegan, and none of them ate sugar. It was pretty strange for a kid to like cereal—most kids didn't even watch commercials anymore—they just streamed the news on their phones. But my mother loved cereal and kept boxes of it in the house when I was young. She would keep old cereal boxes and display them as art in the living room. She especially loved the boxes that had cartoon characters on them. As a kid I didn't understand that these cartoons weren't from a movie or a television show, but were just for the cereal. It didn't make any sense. But my mother loved them. She knew all their names and their histories, and she especially loved the cereals with marbits in them—that's what she called the little freeze-dried marshmallow bits. Kids weren't really allowed to eat cereal, it was thought of as an adult indulgence, like smoking cigarettes or alcohol, but my mother let me taste hers whenever she had a bowl. It was a special thing we would do together before she died. So when I was twenty-one, and finally allowed to go to Cerealand—I applied for a job there, thinking that this was the easiest way I would be able to get to eat all the cereal I wanted.

I am no longer a Marshmallow Boy, I am a Cerealand Mascot. It's a job with a lot more perks. The problem is that it can be a lifetime commitment unless you buy your way out of your contract and pay for the surgery to turn you back to normal. Which is pricey.

Cerealand isn't like other theme parks. It's a park for adults to be childish and relive their youth while still behaving like irresponsible adults. People do drugs in the park, and have sex—they overload on cereal and vomit all over the fake fruity pebble bricks. There is very little about this place that is wholesome and fun.

It wasn't always like this. It was a gradual decline once the founder of the park died and his daughters took over. They realized that, in order to compete with the bigger theme parks like Disneyland and Six Flags, Cerealand was going to have to offer something no one else did.

That's why when you get drafted to be a mascot it's a big decision. It's not like at Disney where you just put on a large, uncomfortable costume and sweat around for hours. They take things a little further at Cerealand. They alter you physically, like genetically. They make you undergo plastic surgery to look more like the cereal mascot you are going to be. The guy who plays Tony the Tiger, for instance, is actually covered in real tiger fur. He has long black stripes tattooed into his skin and he even has tiger ears on the top of his head that wiggle. And you're not allowed to break character, even when you're at home in the dormitories, or in the shower—obviously it's hard to enforce these rules, but if you get caught breaking a rule, your contract is extended without pay. I am always telling myself I really should have read the thing more carefully before I signed it.

I have been Lucky the Leprechaun for almost five

years. I work in Lucky Charms Valley, which is what they call the part of the park that's leprechaun themed. I'm not sure if Lucky Charms was a popular cereal back when cereals were for children, but now it seems like people hate it. No one ever comes to Lucky Charms Valley ever since we started selling Lucky Charms Marshmallow bits by themselves so people could add them to any cereal they want. People dismiss Lucky Charms as just being strangely shaped frosted Cheerios with marshmallows. Which is exactly what they are.

I never wanted to be a Mascot, by the way, that was always her idea.

On my way back to the dorms, I try to avoid looking at any of the people leaving the park. They are all mostly drunk or high and stumbling to the transport vans by the entrance. If you avoid eye contact they usually leave you alone, but it's also the time they are most aggressive. Even though my cereal or the rides in Leprechaun Valley aren't popular at all, I still seem to be a character most of the people recognize. And I tend to get cornered and harassed until I say my catchphrase.

Before I can get through the crowd towards the employee housing, someone stops me. Placing a hand on my shoulder and gripping it with tight slimy fingers. Almost on instinct at this point I say, "You'll never get me lucky charms!"

"Relax, Lucky." A small deep voice croaks out. I

turn and realize it's not a drunk park goer, but instead it's a small man who's been made to look like a slimy frog in a t-shirt and red baseball cap. His skin has been tinted green and his lips are pulled wide so he looks more like a monkfish than a frog. I've seen this face every day for the last five years and I still am shocked and disgusted every single time. I'm serious, it's like someone took a hammer to a sleeping bag full of snails and then made the resulting mess into a face. Plus, the frogman isn't wearing pants, so his slimy frog dick is just barely hovering above the ground.

"Oh, hi Dig," I say. I don't have anything against Dig Em Frog, I just don't like looking at him.

"Lucky," he says, and the way he oozes words out of his elongated frog lips makes me want to punch him. "Have any smokes?"

I hand him a smoke and a match. It's hard for him to hold the cigarette in his mouth.

"Have you seen Sam today m'boy?" I ask him. I try to speak as little as possible since I am required to talk in a stupid cartoon Leprechaun voice. Normally I wouldn't give too much of a shit, but they are more strict about that rule that most of the others. And it's the one I am usually okay with since I don't really need to talk to anyone. I've gotten so used to my inner monologue voice that my dumb-as-fuck Irish stereotype voice always catches me off guard.

"No, she wasn't at her evening performance. I had to do back to back shows man, it was bullshit. I'm not a young frog anymore."

This starts to worry me a little. Insisting we meet up and then flaking on me is very Sam, but missing a performance—missing the ability to do her show? That was not like Sam at all. Dig Em looks at me, I guess he's expecting me to say something but I don't. Then he shrugs and

I watch Dig Em hobble away, it's an awkward mix of a crawl and a hop.

Dig Em was one of the first mascots made for the park—and you can tell. The man who Dig Em used to be was clearly a Little Person before he was turned into a grotesque Frog-like person. He doesn't really look like the Frog on the Cereal Box, he looks more like Gollum from the animated version of Lord of the Rings. Beady little eyes and leathery slimy skin. The only thing that makes people realize he's Dig Em Frog is the fact he wears the same T-shirt, cap and sneakers. If I were him I would have probably killed myself long ago.

But I am not him.

Because I'm late for dormitory check-in I get assigned Milk Duty. The park has a large fountain of milk at the main entrance and every day, the milk sits in the sun and rots and curdles. People will also puke, piss and even fuck in the fountains of milk, depending on how drunk and full of sugar they get. And every day the rotting milk gets funneled into a tank that then has to be drained into a swamp behind the park. Because the milk gets so thick and rancid it can't be done by machines because the gunk sticks to the hoses and gears, so someone has to go down to the swamp area and empty out the giant reservoir of rotten milk by shoveling it into the swamp.

I'm sure there are better ways to do this, but I think that management likes the idea of us having to do it. I mean I get it, I'm sure if I operated this park, I would do the same thing. Or maybe I wouldn't. I don't really know.

When I get down to the Milk Tanks my roommate is already there waiting for me.

"Lucky! Milk Duty tonight? Or just keeping me company?" My roommate's name was once Carl, but he's a Trix Rabbit now—and he's 100% committed to his role.

"Milk Duty," I say

"That's great! I love it when you help me out." Trix hands me a shovel and opens up the Milk Tank. It's like a giant RV trailer that is full of chunks of rancid yogurt. The smell hits me, it's a deep smell of spoiled milk, cum, and vomit and it burns my eyes.

"Holy fuck!"

Trix elbows me in the stomach, "You know we're not allowed to swear" he looks around to make sure no one heard us.

"What d'you do that for!" I yell at him.

"You don't want to break the rules." He tells me. He reaches into a small bag tied around his waist and takes out a handkerchief for my face. I take it from him and wrap it around my nose.

"Will this help with the smell?" I ask.

"Not really, but it sure looks cool though, like we're old-timey train robbers," Trix says as he puts one on his own face and makes little guns with his hands, pointing the guns at me. He winks and grabs a shovel. Trix loves Cerealand. Everything about it. He loves the people, the world, he loves remembering old cereals and knows all about each mascot. He even volunteers for Milk Duty because he just loves helping out. Even though we are total opposites, I am always happy when I get to work with him. He makes me remember the fact that I once loved it here too. But as I am plunging a shovel into a river of rotten milk, that feeling doesn't last.

Trix shovels up a large, almost solid, chunk of milk and tosses it into the swamp.

"So, what did Sam want to talk about?" Trix asks.

"I don't know, she didn't show up" I try to shovel up some milk but it bubbles and releases a burp of toxic breeze into my face and I have to look away.

"That's strange," Trix says

"Not really, Sam is always like this. She makes plans and then forgets about them. She can be a very selfish and forgetful lass." I dig my shovel into the milk and get a decent scoop of it, flinging it over my shoulder towards the swamp. The smell of the milk in the tank is bad, but the smell of the swamp behind us is unbearable. Years of accumulating rotten milk and bile have settled at the bottom and have created a crusty layer of bluegreen botulism at the top.

"That's not right." Trix says as he digs around in the milk muck.

"Yeah, but 'tis her nature, what are ye going to do?" I say. And even though I am saying that, I am feeling annoyed at Sam for blowing me off. And I start thinking about the things I will say to her when I see her next.

"No, that's not what I mean. Look," says Trix. I snap out of my thoughts and look at what the rabbit is pointing at. "Raspberry Red," says the rabbit. At first, I don't see anything. It's dark outside and the inside of the milk container is even darker. But then my eyes adjust, and at first it's nothing. It looks like a spot of red, like the jam in the yogurt before you mix it up. But then it gets closer, it's floating towards us in milk. A small river of red mixed into the white. A few colorful feathers. I pick one up, and I can see the roots, the feather was yanked out, and there is dried blood on it. I don't think anything at this point. I don't know what I am doing or why, but I just go into the vat of milk. The ceiling is low so I have to crawl, the rancid milk getting all over my Leprechaun suit but I don't really care. There are more and more feathers, I crawl faster—the smell isn't even registering to me anymore. I get to the end of the tank and dig my hands into the milky river. I feel around but all I find is more bloodstained feathers.

I met Sam when she started working as a Bar Tender at the Cereal Bar. I would go help her every day after my shift sorting Marshmallow Bits had ended. Sam and I started dating almost right away, she made this place fun for me. Even though by that time I hated cereal, she made cereal less of a hell.

She was the one that proposed the idea that we should become Mascots at the park.

"Think about it," she said "We could make a lot of money and be able to get out of here, move someplace nice. It would just be for four years." She placed a blended drink in front of me.

"Here," she said, "try this."

"But aren't you worried about how they change you? I mean some of these mascots look *fucked* up. Like real freaks. I am not sure how they turn you back to being you" I took a sip from the glass she had placed in front of me. It was thick and red, and tasted like melted jolly ranchers and spit. I coughed it up.

"Ugh, what is this?" I said

"It's my own invention—it's part captain crunch milk, park clamato juice, part vodka, with blended mini peach marshmallows—I call it a Bloody CrunchBerry, what do you think?"

"I think it's disgusting"

"Well, I think this whole bar should actually have cereal themed drinks. It's boring that all we serve is the same shit you'd find at any other bar. I'm going to come up with lots of cool drinks, you'll see."

"Well, they can't be worse than this one." I smiled at her.

"Anyway," she continued, "I'm sure they have that figured out—I doubt they would be allowed to do that to someone without a plan for when they have to change them back."

"What?"

"Becoming a Mascot, I'm sure they have it all figured out."

"I don't know," I said. "I'm happy where we are right now."

"You know what I would do, if I became a mascot," she spoke over me as if she was giving a monologue in a school play. "I'd do something special with this place. Something to make it magical again. You know? I would be an amazing Captain Crunch."

I gave her a look and she crinkled her nose at me to shut me up.

"Who says that the captain has to be a dude? We have female versions of almost all the characters,"

She had a point.

"I would bring the Captain back, I would stop all of the parts of the park that focused on sex and drugs, and I would create a safe place for people to eat cereal, laugh and play games. To be kids again, the way kids *used* to be. Not the fuckwad kids of today, who only care about social crusading and kale, but the kids that used to love the pure fun of having fun. I would put the triplets in a blender, and grind them up into a rice Krispie smoothie and fill the fountain with their goo!" She smiled, swimming laps in her vision of a perfect park.

"Why would you kill the triplets?" I said, half laughing at the image of people in a giant cartoon blender.

"Because they've turned this place into something sad—something wicked, and they don't deserve it. If we were in charge we could help turn it into something wonderful." She smiled at me. "Wouldn't that be amazing?"

"Is that really your end game here? Become a Mascot, kill all the people who run it now, and then take it over? That's the stupidest thing I've ever heard."

She crinkled her nose at me because she knew I loved it. She knew it would soften me up.

"Don't you think I'd make a beautiful Lady Leprechaun?" she crinkled some more, giving me a sly smile. "I think you'd be a very sexy Count Chocula" she nuzzled her face into my neck and made small little neck sucking sounds like a vampire. I held her tight and kissed the top of her head. She made me so happy, and even though I knew becoming a mascot was a terrible idea, I was going to do it. It was what she wanted.

"What are you doing?" Trix asks. "You shouldn't touch those."

"Shut up," I say. There is something wrong here. *These are Sam's feathers, what are they doing in the Milk Vat and why are they covered in blood?* Before I can get a good look, I'm distracted by the lights from the Soggie's security car.

Cerealand didn't use to need its own Security Force, but that was back when the original owner of the park was in charge. Cerealand used to be a friendly theme park, but when only adults would come, it slowly devolved into the shitty-pleasure-island-poor-man's-Amsterdam it is today. When the owner died and his three daughters took it over it, they embraced the only thing the park was good for: making freaks and creating a safe space for fuck ups to act like fuck ups.

Because of this, the park has a sort of private police, The Soggies. If you remember old Captain Crunch commercials, the Soggies were these gross drippy milk monsters that looked like cum creatures. They would try to steal Captain Crunch cereal. Try to make it soggy. But Crunch's cereal would never get soggy, the captain would boast. And so he would defeat the Soggies every time. The owner of the park used to dress up as Captain Crunch when he was alive. When he died, the park retired the Character so that he would be the only Captain Crunch the park would ever have. I used to find it ironic that the park's security was named after creatures that always tried to ruin his cereal. Nowadays I don't really give a shit about anything to do with this place.

The Soggies don't talk much. Or I guess it's more honest to say I've never heard them talk much. Like most of the employees at Cerealand, they have been genetically modified to look more like the characters they are playing, but I'm not sure if they started out as people who have been liquefied, or as piles of milk that have been animated. It doesn't really matter, I guess, either way, they are way gross. I don't like thinking about them more than I have to.

One of the Soggies gets out of his little security car and walks down to the milk tanks by the swamp.

He sees me standing over the feathers and then looks to Trix, who is standing still. Still smiling, waiting for the Soggies to tell him what to do like a good little soldier. I'm sure this is going to be difficult to explain, but the officer doesn't really look at us. He waves his milky arm towards the car. Even though his body is basically liquid, it sticks together like white mercury. I keep waiting for parts of his arm to sling off his body and splash on the ground like wet mud but that doesn't happen. What does happen is two more officers get out of the car and join him by the feathers. They push me out of the way and scoop up all the feathers they can find and without saying a word they walk back up the hill towards their car.

As the last one exits the milk vat I block his path. "Hey, what the hell are you doing?"

He stops and looks right at me, he has to look down to make eye contact with me.

"Where the hell are you taking those?"

The Soggy grabs my arm, it's a freezing cold grip and his hand forms around my arm like an ice cube made of milk. It burns and I yell out. The Soggy smiles at me and stares me down. They don't really have eyes—just eye holes barely formed out of gaps in their milky bodies. Like the eyes of ghosts who are made out of bedsheets. It stops me cold. He lets me go and walks up to join the other Soggies as they get in the car and drive off.

"Something sure fucked happened here, and they are trying to cover it up. Something happened to Sam."

I say to mostly myself, but I guess to Trix as well.

Trix puts a hand on my shoulder.

"She's probably dead, Lucky." he sighs, "And there's really nothing you can do about it right now, so let's get back to work, okay?" he says with a trademark Cerealand smile. He shovels the milk like a cartoon train conductor shoveling coal. Trix really is a piece of shit.

When we get back to the employee dormitories we reek of sour milk. I'm not sure how I was able to keep working, or even how I was able to make it back to my room. The whole night seems like a joke my mind is playing on me. I am having a lot of trouble believing that what has happened has happened. But I also know I don't have any real evidence. I don't really know what happened or if anything even did. Those were her feathers, I know that. I mean, I assume they are. But that could mean anything. Also, I'm very tired and all I really want to do is have a smoke and take a sleep.

"Don't you want to shower?" Trix asks.

I don't listen to him. All I can do is think about Sam and also about having a cigarette.

"The whole room is going to smell Lucky. Please. At least take those clothes off."

I am still coated in milk when I lay on my bed and stare at the ceiling fan. If I look at it in the right way, it looks as if the fan is standing still and the room is spinning. *It's spinning so fast.* I keep thinking about tonight, why did she contact me out of the blue after so long? What did she want to tell me? And why were bloody feathers in the vat of milk? *Faster and faster.* Were the feathers bloody or am I just adding that now?

"Lucky, the room smells like vomit. Please."

Staring at the fan makes me feel like I'm in a tornado. It makes me feel like I might get flung off into space. *Faster and faster.* I make up my mind to accept the fact that I'm being paranoid, and that logically, probably nothing bad has happened to Sam, and that she probably just blew me off. This makes me feel better, because it means I don't really have to do anything about it.

I get an erection but I can't jerk off with Trix in the room so I close my eyes and pretend to be asleep until I actually am.

I dream that I am on a train. I'm in a compartment with three other people. One of them is a large fish, I think. Like a fish head but with a white mustache and a captain's hat. There is someone who looks like a tiny doll version of my father, who is reading an old comic book. There is also a woman, sitting across from me. I can't see her face because I am seeing the dream through her eyes. And I see myself, as a passenger on the train. I can see through her eyes, that I am asleep in my seat. I can't control which way I look, I can't turn her head. I just stare at myself sleeping. I look like my old self, my pre-Leprechaun self. At least I think I do. I don't really remember what I used to look like, but I know it's me that I'm looking at. My face is strained and my eyes are closed tight. There is sweat forming on my forehead and sides of my neck. My breathing is labored and short.

In the dream, on this train, I am staring at myself have a nightmare. The woman, whose eyes I'm seeing this through, is just staring at me. The other people in the compartment are minding their own, the fish man is eating a rice cake, and my tiny doll-father is still reading his comic book. But the woman just keeps staring at me, so I am forced to keep staring at me. My lips are pressed tight, turning a marshmallow white from lack of blood flow. My eyes are darting like trapped bees behind my eyelids. Whatever it is I'm having a nightmare about, it's terrifying me. I want to wake myself up but I can't move, I can't do anything except watch myself through the woman's eyes. She doesn't blink.

Something loud wakes me up. But by the time I'm actually fully awake, it's quiet again and I don't know what that sound was and I try to go back to sleep. But I can't, I'm awake now and I have to piss. I sit up and notice a puddle of gooey milk slowly creeping through the crack below the door. Trix isn't in his bed—he's usually up way before me. The loud noise again. It's a knock, I realize. Someone is knocking on the door. It sounds like an ominous knock. You know the kind. My head throbs. Why do I always wake up feeling like I died the night before? Not a bad death, but like a peaceful death, you know. One that I was praying for and finally arrived but was then ripped away from me.

"'Tis open," I say, and slowly sit up and grab my Lucky the Leprechaun hat from the nightstand.

The door to my room opens up and two Soggies come in and clear a path. I can tell who it is simply by the scent in the air. Even though my room stinks from Milk Duty, her perfume overtakes it. I can't really describe the scent, but I'll try. It's kind of like the smell of an old small bookstore, if you remember those, the kind that sells vintage used books. But imagine if all the old books had been soaked in vanilla and lavender oils and left to dry in the sun. And then you'd have to imagine spilling a bottle of deer piss on the floor of that bookshop. And then closing all the windows so there is no breeze and the thickness of the smell slogs like gravy down through your nose. Something like that.

Back in my room, the Soggies stand perfectly still as she saunters in on thigh-high, heeled boots. Her dark purple hair is braided and almost touches the floor. She has a tight red leather trench coat on, and her trademark tiny yellow hat rests on her head like Jughead's paper crown. Her eyes are almost as big as her giant cartoonish tits, which bounce like beach balls on her disproportionally tiny body. She looks like a sexed up hentai version of an elf.

She pulls out one of the small chairs in the room, moves it to the foot of my bed and kneels on it, resting her arms on the chair back. It's a very strange way to sit in a chair and it makes me uneasy.

"Hello, Lucky." She says. "Mind if I have one of these?"

She reaches under my mattress, casually—and pulls out a pack of cigarettes that I keep hidden under there. The fact that she knew exactly where to find them doesn't sit well with me.

"We should talk," she says. As she puts the cigarette in her mouth she nods towards the lighter that is on the bedside table, but she doesn't make a move for it. I know she is expecting me to light her cigarette for her, but I am not in the mood for these fucking mind games. I don't give a shit if she's my boss and can fire me, or worse. I am not in a hurry to start my day listening to this crazy elf try to cover up something so fucked up, she felt the need to come and explain it to me first thing in the morning. I know whatever it is she says is going to be bullshit and that means that something bad probably did happen to Sam, and that I'll probably have to do something about it. And I'm not in a rush to start that shit. So I just stare at her and then back to the lighter. And it's a stalemate, neither of us making a move and she just sits there, clove cigarette in her dumb mouth, waiting and smiling the patient smile of an alligator.

Cerealand was founded by a man named Cornelius Ellis. He created it because he has assumed that people all over the world loved cereal as much as he did. In the first few years that Cerealand existed, it was apparently very fun. It was really more of a place dedicated to nostalgia than just cereal, although cereal was the anchoring theme. Adults who had grown up in the 80s and 90s would come to the park and become kids again. They stuffed their faces with cereal and played on old Nintendo systems and drank discontinued sodas like OK and Jolt. Old Saturday morning cartoons would blast on screens all over the park. Cornelius loved the idea of everyone being able to be a kid every once in a while. Even though he was the owner of the park he still insisted on being one of the Mascots. He grew his beard out and dyed it white, and put on a captains outfit. He would welcome the park goers everyday, and put on shows for them. This was all way before my time. I never got to meet Captain Crunch in person.

Cornelius had three daughters, Sandra, Chelsea, and Poe, who took over for him when he died. And that's when the Cerealand that we all know today became what it is. It was the Krispie Triplets, as they are known, that realized that for all the good their father wanted to create, what he had actually built wasn't a childlike wonderland for adults, but a rundown playground for ugly-people debauchery. The sisters had grown up in the park, and they knew that most people who came to Cerealand would just get high in the parking lot, sneak flasks of booze onto the rides, and break into the Crunch berry fields to have sex after hours. That was the Cerealand the girls knew. So when they took it over, they not only embraced that element of the park—they amplified it. Pretty much the only real idea of Cornelius's to have made it through the revamping of the park was the surgical enhancements for the Mascots. But unlike the other mascots in the park, the Krispie Triplets didn't make themselves look anything like the Snap, Crackle and Pop elves. I hadn't met Snap or Crackle, but if Pop was any indication of what her sisters looked like, The triplets looked more like cartoon pixie dominatrices. In fact, the only real way you could tell that she was even supposed to be a Cereal Mascot was because of the small yellow hat on her head.

Pop was intense. She had large purple eyes that matched her hair, but no pupils. Just large purple dots in the middle of her wide, white eyes. And I keep staring at them, as she knelt in that chair at the foot of my bed, unblinking her large purple dots. I am not sure if ten minutes have passed between us or ten seconds but the silence is fucking irritating me, so I buckle and light her cigarette.

"Lucky," she says, "I just wanted to make sure you're doing okay."

I just stare at her. I don't feel like talking.

"We just want you to know that here at Cerealand, we're a family Lucky. And families look out for each other."

The ash on her cigarette is getting long. She doesn't ash it. She just lets it sit there.

"They trust each other." she goes on, "And I need to know we can trust each other."

The smoke is wafting into her open eyes but it doesn't faze her. The cigarette is now more than half ash. Just resting on the end of her cherry like dried up dog shit. I can't focus on anything she is saying. I just keep looking at the cigarette, waiting for her to ash it. *Willing* her to ash it.

"I want you to know that if you have any issues or concerns about anything you come to me…" She goes on about something else, I think, she keeps talking but I can see the ash eating the paper, devouring the cigarette like a virus eating away at a body in a bad horror movie. The cigarette, almost entirely ash now, is somehow holding strong. I am in awe of this.

"Are we clear?"

I look up from her mouth and into her purple dots. Apparently, she has made a point she needs me to agree with, but I wasn't paying attention. So I just stare at her, and I give her a little nod.

Pop smiles and that small movement sets the ash free. The ash falls like dandruff snowflakes onto my bed. I smile. Sweet relief.

"I'm glad we understand each other," she says. Before she leaves she does the strangest thing, she stops short and takes my hat off, she smooths my hair over and she holds up a finger to my face while squinting an eye. "Say, 'Part of a Complete Breakfast' for me."

I do. I don't like that I do, but I do. And she smiles. "Thanks," she says, and walks out of my room.

Dig Em Frog looks up at me from his lily pad, "Smart kid." he says.

He is slathering suntan lotion on the top of his bald slimy head. He says he needs to protect himself from the solar flares, even though sunblock isn't something that protects you from that, he lathers it on like it is liquid skin. The mixture of the lotion and his gelatinous frog sweat makes it look like he is covered in hair gel. "You don't want to mess with Pop, she's a froggin' psycho." Dig Em says froggin' when he wants to say fuckin' since cursing isn't allowed on the job. "You're a good kid," the frog oozes from his wound of a mouth. "Good kids don't last in Cerealand"

I want to punch him in the face. The kind that would hurt my hand as much as his face. Not because of what he says, but the way he says it. The way he says anything, really, makes me want to just destroy myself punching him.

"I've been here for over nine years," I tell him.

"Yeah," he says, not listening to me, "You'll be lucky if you survive here." he laughs to himself, "You'll be lucky, get it?" Dig Em's exposed slimy dick dips in and out of the pond water where he spends most of the day. I feel like I need to say something so as not to just sit there looking at him. So I ask him about Sam. Not because

I think he will have anything of value to say, but that's where my mind is right now. Thinking about Sam.

"Yesterday, when you had to take over for Sam's show, who told you she wasn't going to go on?"

Dig Em doesn't look at me when he speaks. Or maybe he does, but his eyes are too small and far apart for me to notice.

"No one." He croaks, "She just didn't show up. The crowd was all seated and waiting. Evening show, so there were plenty of drunks. After fifteen minutes of them getting restless, I just jumped in and did my show. It was horrible, they were not in there to see me and boy did they let me know it."

I was hoping asking the Frog would have been more helpful.

"Did you see her at all yesterday?"

"I spend most of my time here," Dig Em pats his lily-pad, "And when's the last time one of the main Mascots were in this part of the park?"

He was right. Our cereals had been deemed the least popular over the years and we were located at what could only be considered the skid row of Cerealand. Because you can add Lucky Charms Marshmallows to any cereal as well as the fact that Sugar Crisp World was at the center of the park—Lucky Charms and Honey Smacks have kind of become obsolete. The 'Honey Smacks Ribbit Exhibit' was made to be a pre-school daycare area when the park originally opened, where families could bring their little ones to catch frogs and touch salamanders while the parents went out and enjoyed the park. It was like a Reptile Petting Zoo. But I've heard that even when the park did attract the odd family, back then, this part of the park was always a dead zone. Dig Em's shack was still covered with the same colorful paintings of frogs and toads and lizards from when it was a petting zoo. There is a really creepy chameleon that is painted with a rainbow color pattern I guess to show that it can change into many colors, but it just ends up looking like a shitty tie-dye lizard. I hate it, but it's by far my favorite thing to look at when I'm at Dig Ems pond. Honey Smacks' world is right next to Lucky's Land of Leprechauns, at the very outer edge of the park, by the electric fence that separates the old discontinued rides from the operating part of Cerealand—most people really don't bother with this part of the park which works for us just fine. It's become the part of my job I hate the least. But this morning there have been Soggies driving by, checking in. Maybe I'm being paranoid. After all, I actually don't know anything, and I have no real idea how to go about finding anything out. So what do I have to worry about? They have nothing on me.

Although what *did* happen to Sam? Why wasn't she at her show, and were those her feathers I found in the milk? And if so, why were they covered in blood? Well, not covered in blood. I shouldn't start exaggerating this early on. They had some blood on them. But what did that even mean? For all I know some sick piece of shit booked her for a show and things got a little rough, she lost a few feathers. Some kinky fuck yanked them out for a souvenir and then, what, he dropped them in the milk fountain? Did that make sense? Or maybe they're quills. Right? That's a thing. Quills. Maybe.

"You've been staring into space mouthing words to yourself for, like, five minutes," says Dig Em.

I look at him and pull out a cigarette from under my Leprechaun hat. It's my last one.

"So what?" I say.

Dig Em sticks out his slimy sausage casing tongue and snatches the cigarette out of my mouth and lights it for himself.

"So what? So I've been trying to have a conversation with you. And you're being a froggin' jerk."

He's right. But all I do is stare at him while he smokes my last cigarette.

"I'm going to find out who did this, Dig. I don't really care why they did it, I just want to find out what happened and who did it. And then I'm going to kill whoever that is."

Dig Em blows smoke rings in the air while he dips his dick in and out of the water.

"Whatever," he says.

I decide to go for a walk. Stretch the little leprechaun legs. But I have no idea where I'm walking to because I'm still mumbling things in my head to myself. When I look up to figure out where the fuck I am I realize that I'm in Main Street Cerealand, which is mostly empty.

It still has its generous handful of stoned customers, stumbling through the streets and waiting in line for the rides, but there are a lot fewer Mascots. Usually, the street would be full of them, entertaining the guests, handing out shots of crushed Golden Grahams Tequila. I usually avoid this part of the park because I always assume it will be crowded.

At the entrance to the park, where you'd normally be greeted by the more recognizable of the mascots, are two characters I don't recognize. Boxy looking things, waddling around like fat baby ducks. I have no idea who they could be, but they are far enough away that I don't really get a good look at them. I don't really care that much. I see Grapefellow and wave him over. Grapefellow is a mascot from a discontinued cereal—the park has a lot of old mascots. Since the park wasn't owned by any one cereal company, the characters were licensed from places like Kellogg's, Post, and General Mills. Discontinued cereals were much cheaper to license, and played into the idea that the park was more for adults who remembered this kind of nostalgia that most young people didn't care about. I felt bad for the old mascots. They still had to undergo the surgery but most people didn't care about them. Grapefellow looked hollowed out and thin like a scarecrow made of purple pixie sticks. His skin was a pale blue and he had a thick curly-cue mustache that was coated in sprinkles. He looked nothing like the mascot from the cereal, who was just a British war pilot who wore purple clothing.

"Hey Grapes"

He looks over at me, unsure of who I was.

"It's Lucky," I say. And gave him a little wave.

Grapefellow is old, way older than anyone else working at the park. But he hadn't been working there for that long. The rumor was that he was a homeless man that the Triplets kidnapped and turned into Grapefellow because they had the rights to this character just sitting and collecting dust. But I think his backstory is much sadder than that. I always imagine he has a wristwatch that he's always rubbing with his thumb and forefinger in his hands, never wearing it on his wrist. It's not a fancy watch, I tell myself, but it's also not something a homeless man would ever own. I imagine that there is a sad backstory to that watch, something that led him here to this miserable job. I am pretty sure there is, and one day I want to think up a good one. And then tell Grapefellow about it.

"Lucky!" he says. "This is a rare sighting indeed! What takes you away from your pot of gold?"

I ignore his question. I've always been very talented at ignoring questions.

"Who are those two, by the entrance?" I ask. I'm also good at asking questions. Almost as good as I am at ignoring them.

"Oh, those are the new arrivals. The Triplets brought them on about a week ago, I believe. Strange looking chaps aren't they?"

I try to take a better look at the two but they are too far away.

"I'm not really sure what cereal they belong to," says Grapes, "but they took over greeting duties this week. I think that they are German spies."

"I can't imagine the Tiger was happy about that." I smile. The thought of that showboat not getting to be the face of the park anymore is nice. It's a mean thought, sure. I'm a jerk for having it. But I have it.

"Sir Tony? Oh, I'm afraid I haven't seen Sir Tony in quite some time." Grapefellow looks back over his shoulder. Then bends over to whisper to me, his breath smells of cocoa puff gin,

"The Baron, you see, is all around and he has ears everywhere my lad. He lives off of the fear, he eats it, you see. The Baron has his eyes to the ground and his ears in the sky. He got the Tiger. He got the Toucan. He'll get you too."

"Wait, what about the Toucan? Do you know where Sam is?"

Grapefellow isn't looking at me, he's just looking at the two Square mascots at the front entrance.

"The Baron." he says "The Baron is behind it all. They were once pure, but now they are filthy, they are filthy and the Baron punishes filth. He makes them even dirtier. He makes them *scum!* The Baron will eat the ears right off your head!"

"Jesus Christ man, it's a simple question. Do you know where Sam is?"

Grapefellow stares at the sky and frowns.

"You can never see the moon in this place." He takes out a flask and tips what's left into his mouth.

Before I can respond to him, Grapefellow is walking back towards his ride, 'The Grapest Caper' it's a ride that's a lot like the Haunted Mansion at Disneyland, only it's about a murder at Grape Manor. It's a terrible ride. No one ever rides it. Which is why Grapefellow can get away with being drunk most of the day. I decide that Grapefellow isn't a good lead to follow. He's certifiably batshit and I am pretty sure he was just rambling and drunk.

I stare back at the two square people at the front gates. There is something about them that gives me the creeps.

I look around to try to find someone else to talk to, but I don't find anyone I recognize.

That's not entirely true. I see Trix, but I don't want to talk to him so I try to look like I'm busy, and I accomplish this by furrowing my brow and looking distracted as he walks towards me.

But it doesn't work.

"Hey, roomie. You were really tossing and a-turnin' last night, huh?"

"Wha the fuck are you talking about?"

"Are you crazy using that word! We're on Main Street for Captain's sake! Plus, you know I don't like it when you use that kind of language even at the dorms."

I don't say anything. I keep furrowing my brow. I've committed.

"Anyway, thanks to your sleep talking I barely got up in time for Marbit Picking."

"God Forbid you miss a morning of Marbit picking. You have to loosen the fuck up."

"Lucky! Language!"

"You have to learn to relax."

"What the heck are you talking about Lucky? You're the most stressed out person I know."

I give him a fuck you look.

"Why are you looking at me like that?" he says.

I don't say anything. I just keep giving him that look.

"Listen, just do something about your nightmares. It's keeping me up and if it doesn't stop I'm going to ask to switch roommates. I'm really sorry."

Trix walks away, I can tell that this confrontation was hard on him. He doesn't like having to stand up for himself, or be mean to anyone, so I know even small confrontations like this make him sick for hours. That's a silver lining at least.

"Trix," I call out as he hops away, he turns to me "you're a real *piece* of shit." I lean on the word Piece for some reason. It sounds very strange coming out of my mouth.

Trix stares at me, then shakes his head and continues to hop down Main Street. Trix would be the fourth roommate that has kicked me out in the last few years. And I guess that says a lot about me. I guess I have to take a real good look at how I've been choosing roommates.

Before Trix is out of ear I call out.

"Hey."

He turns, shrugs at me.

I yell out, "Trix, can I ask you something?"

He hops back over to me.

"You're pretty good on your cereal history. Does the name The Baron mean anything to you?"

"The Baron? That's why you called me over?"

"Yeah. Grapefellow was talking about it."

"I thought you were going to apologize for calling me a P of S!"

"What?—no. I just need help figuring out this clue, I guess it's a clue? It's not really anything yet."

"Here's a clue for you Lucky, you're a terrible friend, you're selfish and self-involved and you make me hate it here, and I love it here. So start looking for another place to live."

He hops away, now completely upset at me. I stare at him hop.

"That's not a clue," I say. But Trix is gone and I say this to no one.

I don't want to think about what might have happened to my ex-girlfriend, but I don't want to think about having to move dorm rooms even more than I don't want to think about Sam. So I start to come up with all these scenarios where Sam is fine and I am overacting to the bloody feathers. I come up with these scenarios because it helps me feel okay with being so helpless in this situation. For the last four years, I have been saving up the money I would need to buy myself out of my contract. It's not an easy thing to do because Cerealand garnishes your wages for literally everything. Cost of living, food, operation to turn you into a Cereal Mascot, housing, it goes on and on. So in order to have saved up the money I need to buy myself out of this place I have had to opt out of having a social life or any fun at all. Other than the occasional pack of clove cigarettes, I haven't spent a hard dime on anything frivolous in almost half a decade. I don't go to the restaurants or bars anymore, I don't visit the Strip Clubs or the Sex Shows. I stick to my job, and the employee dorms and cafeteria. Because of this, however, I have forgotten the layout of this place, there are buildings and rides I've never even seen before, and so I have no idea where to start looking, and even if I did, I'm not sure I have any idea of what I'm looking for.

I wander around the side streets of the park. Not wanting to go back to the room and deal with an annoyed Trix. Not knowing where to go. I guess I know what I'm doing, but I look surprised when I end up outside the Toucan Tower of Power. An S&M Dungeon themed ride that featured Sam. It's a popular show and it's close to the main stage and Frosted Lakes, the Tony the Tiger water park portion of Cerealand. But whereas normally these are the busiest parts of the park, or at least used to be, they seem oddly deserted and quiet. Even the neon signs around the rides seem dimmer. But that's stupid. It's stupid to think this. I'm just trying to set a mood in my head. I'm sure the neon is as bright as it ever was, and the reason it looks so empty is because it's closing time and everyone is leaving the park. But I know that's a damn lie I'm telling myself. I can tell that something is sour. I stand there. There is a large statue of Toucan Sam outside, in the courtyard where I'm standing. It doesn't look like Sam, who is, *or was*, a sexy girl version of the Mascot, no it looks more like the actual cartoon character on the box of cereal. His large multi-colored beak stretched outwards like an arrow. Pointing me towards the direction of Sugar Alley—the Red Light District of the park. If this were a comic book, or an old detective movie, that statue would be a clue, the beak pointing me towards my next step in the case. But it's just a statue. A sign telling people where to go. Peeking my head around the corner, the walls of Sugar Alley are still alive with a bright red glow. Even though the rides were closed for the day, Sugar Alley stayed open all night; this is when what most people called *the real fun* would start. Before I can decide if I want to walk the alley, I see one of those square mascots from before, it's across the courtyard, near the center milk fountain. I still can't get a good look, so I start walking towards the fountain.

When I get closer I see that the square thing is not alone. Two Soggies are with it, guiding it somewhere. The square thing is walking awkwardly and needs a lot of help. It's like the Soggies are helping a fat, square, drunk child get home. I'm small and it's dark so it's easy for me to follow them. I'm not sure why I think I should be quiet, discreet—but I guess I don't want to call attention to myself or have to talk to them. I just want to know what's going on. It's a good distraction. They are walking towards the security building, maybe the new mascot fucked up and is in trouble. I guess there's nothing interesting about that. But I hide behind a tree and wait for them to walk into the light to get a better look at the new guy. But they walk right past the security building, towards the back gate.

The night is very cold, and there still isn't a moon, so it's very dark now that we are away from the lights of the park. The Soggies are still guiding this thing, through the field behind the parking lot. I have no idea where they are going, but I've committed this far—it would be silly to turn back now. The Soggies are talking to each other but I can't hear them clearly, I'm too far back. The grass is tall here, and wet, but I still need to crouch as I try to catch up with them and not be seen. They are walking pretty slowly, but I still need to be careful when I walk. Timing my steps with those of the Soggies, with the wet slap of their milky feet on the ground so they can't hear me. But now I'm close enough that I can make out their conversation. I normally don't get to hear them talk. For most of the time I've been at the park I imagined that the Soggies were just a sort of hive mind. Stoic and cold, brainless bastards that just did as they were commanded. I guess I never took the time to see them as anything other than gross piles of living milk.

"You are so full of shit." says one of the Soggies, "You're telling me you never paid for it before Cerealand? You're fucking crazy."

"No. You're fucking disgusting." The other Soggie is walking the Square thing by the arm. The first Soggie isn't helping.

"How am I disgusting?"

"You can help me with this thing, by the way, we're supposed to be guiding this guy together."

"You're doing great. And answer the question, how am I disgusting?"

"Paying for sex is gross. Even here, where it's all supposed to be part of the show, there is something so low brow about it, so sleazy to me."

"You've never taken a girl out to a nice dinner and a show in order to fuck her, I guess."

"That's totally different."

"Why? Because in your version you spend the money but might not get the sex?"

"No. Because in my version, if she sleeps with me, she is doing it because she wants to, not because I am paying for it. A girl only wants to sleep with a guy if she loves him."

"That's so horribly misogynistic. Girls like sex and cash and no strings attached as much as any person."

"You're not going to convince me that paying for sex is anything but sad and pathetic."

"Your loss. Now seriously help me, this guy can barely walk."

"This guy is barely a guy. What the fuck are they doing to these things anyway?"

It's kind of amazing to me to hear this conversation. I had always believed that the Soggies didn't talk to each other and that they just kind of followed blindly like worker bees or the Goombas from the Super Mario Brother's Movie. The one with John Leguizamo. One of the Goombas in the movie was supposed to be Toad from the video game, who in the game was a little child-like man who wore a colorful mushroom cap as a hat. In the movie, he was a Goomba, like I said. And the Goombas were these dumb as rocks soldiers for King Koopa. They would look intimidating but also harmless and didn't have any distinguishing personality traits. That's what I had always thought the Soggies were like. But now that I'm up close I realize that they are all unique, with personalities and attitudes. They all seem to be male, or at least these two are male. I'm kind of blown away by this new revelation. It kind of makes me question everything I think I know. And it makes me feel sorry for them. Also, it makes me sad that Super Mario Brothers didn't do well enough to get a sequel.

The Soggies stop and take a look at their companion. I carelessly walk towards them, lost in thought, obsessed now, that they have normal conversations. I catch myself, though, and so I crouch down low, getting a better look, at least at the square mascot's back. It's definitely a Mascot—it's got white gloves and big cartoony feet. Its back is bumpy and uneven. And it's perfectly square. It's wrapped in a blanket so I can't really tell too much else.

"Can this thing understand us?" One of the Soggies says, he is staring right at it.

"It has eyes, it's looking right at you, I think it can understand you."

"How about it freak? Can you understand us?"

The Square tries to nod, but it doesn't have a neck.

"I think it's trying to say something."

"Take the gag out, we're far enough away from the park."

I see one of the guards remove a cloth gag and toss it to the ground. The voice that comes out of the square guy is gurgled. Like is he was talking with a mouth full of hot soup.

"Cold."

"What is he saying?"

"He's saying that he's cold I think. Is that it freak? You cold?"

"Cold," the thing says again.

"He's cold." Says the Soggie carrying him.

"The fuck you want me to do about it?"

"I don't know, give him an extra blanket."

"This is my blanket. I brought it because I knew it was going to be cold. It's not my fucking fault no one else is prepared."

"You're the only one who thought to bring blankets, so let's use them!"

"I already gave the thing one of my blankets. I'm not giving it another one. Plus it's all wet and damp with milk because I've been wearing it. It's not going to keep him warmer." The Soggie wearing the blanket takes the square by the arm and yanks him forward. Annoyed that he has to work now. The Square thing is struggling to keep the pace of the pissed off Soggie. He is fumbling and trembling.

"Cold!" he says.

"Jesus fuck, either give him the blanket or gag him again."

Blanket Soggie stops and turns. He lets go of square guy's hand and stares at the other Soggie.

"Fine, goddamn it. Fine. Here, if you want him to stop crying then you swaddle the baby."

He tosses his blanket over. The other Soggie catches it in the air, but the blanket is heavy and it flops to the floor.

"Jesus this thing is soaked."

"I fucking told you, I've been wearing it all day. And I'm made of milk."

"Whatever, we're almost there. I think this will keep him a little warmer till we get him to the club." The second Soggie, the one who cares about the thing being cold or not, walks up to it with the wet blanket. He looks at it, I can still only see its back. "What do you think they do with these things down there?" He is about to put the blanket on. The thing is shivering now. Leaning his awkward square body toward the blanket.

"Not my pay grade to give a shit."

The Square thing seems happy with this second blanket and they start walking again. Which is good because I've been kneeling in this very uncomfortable way that was making my legs fall asleep. My toes are already pins and needles.

I follow them again as they head deeper into the woods, towards a small dirt path. But the Square guy is starting to slow down, walk funny. Funnier than he already walks, I mean. Like he's sick.

The guards notice this, too, because they stop. They step back as if something is really wrong. I realize I am really close and that if they look over to where I'm crouching they could probably see me, or at least my hat. The grass is much shorter here by the dirt path. Luckily they are focused on whatever is happening to Mr. Squarepants over there.

"What's wrong with him?"

"I have no idea. You think it was the procedure?"

"Don't think so," says the other Soggie, "I've never seen anyone react to it like this. This guy looks like he's about to shit blood out his mouth!"

The Square thing starts to howl. A painful howl, like an old dog being forced through a garbage disposal. Like really shoved in there against his will. It's a horrible sound. The Soggies step back, they are frozen in place, staring at this thing as it screams. *Plop*. Something wet and chunky drops onto the ground. Then more plop sounds. It's like someone is emptying a bucket of oatmeal onto a wet carpet. The thing is shrieking now, but all I can hear is *plop, plop, plop*.

The Soggies stand there as this thing starts to melt under the wet blanket. Pieces of it just sliding off its body, landing in bloody clumps on the grass. This all happens in less than five minutes, or maybe it's been an hour. I feel like I've been crouching in wet grass forever. But I stay still. I try not to breathe.

The Soggies stand over the mess. The Square guy is now just a puddle on the floor.

"Fuck!" Says one of the guards. "We are so fucked!"

"What the hell happened to him!?"

"I don't know! How the fuck would I know that?"

"Well, what do we do?"

The first guard shakes his head. He looks up at the sky. It's clear he is not liking the fact that he has to make the decision. He looks at the goopy mess and then back at the other Soggie.

"Nothing."

"What?"

"We're doing nothing. We just go to the club and tell them he didn't make it through the procedure. That we never picked him up."

"You think they'll buy that?"

"I don't know man. But I don't have any other ideas."

They stand there for a few more minutes and then they head up the dirt path. Once I am sure they aren't coming back, I get up and walk over to get a better look. What's left of the mascot is a soupy mess of blood and cereal mush. I can't really tell what this thing was supposed to be before he melted. One of its little beady eyes floats on top of the goop, I stare at it. I think maybe I can recognize the eye. But I can't. I'm too busy dealing with this eye idea, that I almost miss it. I almost completely miss the red bandana that's sticking out, like a dried bloody Kleenex, from a clump of what looks like wet cardboard and tendons. Even though it's coated in a slimy substance I can tell what it is. That red bandana was on logos all over the fucking park. It is the trademark of the main mascot of Cerealand, like McDonald's arches, or Mickey's ears. Even though it's covered in brown blood, the trademark Raspberry Red of the bandana shines through and I would recognize it anywhere. It belonged to the Tiger.

"Who's your favorite cereal mascot?" Sam was in bed with me, both my legs pinned under her leg. She was walking her fingers through my eyebrows, tickling the top part of my face.

"I don't know," I said, "I don't really have one."

"What? That's stupid. You're an idiot. Everyone who works here should have a favorite."

I was thinking of them, trying to run the list through my mind. It was hard to remember the versions of the mascots from the boxes when I was a kid, all I could picture when I thought of them now was the grotesque mutant mascots from the park.

"You want to know what mine is?" She asked me, tired of waiting for me to answer her.

"I know who your favorite is," I said.

"Or really?" She had this way of smiling, it was strange. It was like a little devil, like the smile a cartoon villain gives the camera when their plan is working out. It was like the smile the Grinch makes in the animated version of How The Grinch Stole Christmas. But she pulled it off, I don't know how but she made that deranged smile cute and flirty. She was giving me the ol' grinch smile.

"Yeah, it's obvious. You wear that dumb red bandana every day."

"It's not dumb," she smiled "It's grrrrrr--"

I covered her mouth with my hand, and muffled

her voice before she could finish the word. She laughed and licked the palm of my hand to get me to pull back my arm.

"When we become mascots, are you just going to run away with that volleyball playing pussy?"

She pulled my hand away from her mouth and straddled me. "Don't worry, idiot," she said.

"You're not getting rid of me that easy."

And that got me thinkin', who would want the Toucan out of the picture? What would they gain? And now the Tiger—why the Tiger!? He's the face of the park. Something is rotten. The whole fucking situation is starting to smell like old piss to me. Those Soggies, they were headed somewhere with that thing. Whatever it was. And why did that thing have on Tony's bandana. Was it even Tony's bandana though, we sell those fucking things in every gift shop at the park. But then why hasn't anyone seen the Tiger? At least that's what Grapefellow says, and I guess I haven't seen him either. But can I trust a doddering old fuck like Grapes? And what was all that shit he said about the Baron? Something fucked is going on here. I know the Triplets are somehow involved but I can't take them on myself. Or prove a goddamn fucking thing. And taking on Pop, that would be hard. I would have to come up with a plan, get help, have an end goal. But I just want to go to sleep, you know? You ever get so tired that you can't sleep? Like your mind won't stop with the thinking. The goddamn thoughts keep coming. What the fuck is happening at Cerealand and where are all the mascots and what the fuck was that thing that melted, fucking *melted*, in the woods, and does any of that have anything to do with Sam? The worst part is I don't really want to do this. Figure it out, I mean. I'm not a detective, I'm not qualified to be looking into any of this. Like at all. And I hadn't really talked to Sam in a long time. It's not like I owed her anything. I guess it's morbid curiosity to find out exactly what happened, plus, I guess I want to make sure I didn't have anything to do with it. I don't want to feel guilty or worse, be blamed for anything. If anything did happen. I guess that's a selfish and ugly thing to have been my motivation, but what can I do? What's your take?"

The young girl at the cereal bar just stares at me. I realize I have been aggressively talking at this girl and freaking her out.

After a minute of her standing still and simultaneously trying to both avoid looking at me and not break eye contact out of fear that I will stab her, I end the silence and ask for a Bloody CrunchBerry.

She places it in front of me and I just let it sit there.

"You know who invented this drink?"

She doesn't answer. She gives me a weak smile and walks to the other side of the bar. She is terrified. I give her the stink eye. I just like that I'm making someone nervous. I don't get to do that as much, not since I was turned into a living cartoon. I imagine my thoughts are like cartoon bubbles floating over my stupid leprechaun hat. And that anyone can read them.

"You gonna drink that, or you just gonna stare at it?" A voice cuts through my thought bubble. Popping it like a balloon.

I don't need to look up, I know who that low grisly voice belongs to. But I do look up, and I notice him sitting at the corner table. He is draped in thick course hair, brown as chestnuts, his bold and muscular legs elegantly sausaged into fishnet stockings and an elaborate leather daddy outfit tries its very best to contain the massive, grisly bulk that is Sugar. His snout pokes out of a leather mask, as do his cartoon bear ears that stick out from the top of his head.

"Just going to stare at it." I say "I hate cereal."

Sugar gets up and saunters up to the seat next to me and inhales my drink. He wears long fake eyelashes that goop together from heavy mascara. His eyes are bloodshot yellow. He pops a cigar the size of French baguette into his mouth.

"Does the gentleman have a light?" he asks.

His snout is bulky and he holds the cigar through the zipper in his mask. I take out my zippo and light him up. The young girl at the bar looks like she's about to say something to the giant bear about how he's not allowed to smoke, but she thinks better of it and keeps to her side of the bar.

"Still sober?" he growls

"Still an asshole?" I don't look at him when I talk to him. I just stare straight ahead.

He licks up some of the waffle crisp bits that are still stuck in his chest hair. I realize that he probably has been listening to everything I was just saying to that poor young bartender. And he confirms this.

"So, I was just listening to everything you were just saying to that poor young bartender," he says.

"So," I say, "you gonna be cool about this, or are we going to have a problem?"

He doesn't say anything. I double down.

"Because fuck you Sugar Bear, I'm going to find out what the hell is happening around here and you can either get on the train or lay down on the tracks bitch—cause this choo-choo is going to fuck your face." I stare ahead, but I can see him through the corner of my eye. I'm being bold here and taking a chance. Sugar smiles, the kind of smile a lion might give a mouse who is trying to pick a fight with him. Even though he is five times my size I am just stupid enough to think I could get in a few good scratches to the eyes if it came to that. Fuck up at least one of those eyes.

He reaches over and grabs a bottle of Cinnamon Toast Schnapps from behind the bar and then pours it into his zipper hole. The sound of him gulping down the thick, snotlike booze, sounds like a toilet getting plunged. I think how if I *am* going to scratch at his eyes, now might be a good time to do it. His left eye is closest to me. I am thinking about how much time I would need to do it, to gauge out his eye, if I was really dedicated and focused on the task. If I really *believed* in myself. He finishes pouring out the bottle into his fat face and licks up the excess schnapps from the counter. He looks satisfied. Then he puts his hand on top of my hat, patting it like if it were my head.

"Come on little man, let's get out of here." He wobbles towards the door, not really waiting to see if I am following him or not. He speaks over his shoulder at me as we walk outside.

"You're not going to like this, but you'll probably want to see it."

Sugar Bear is a lumberjack of a man, yet walks with the decidedly confident strut of a 1960's femme fatale. I notice for the first time he wears black high heeled shoes with bright red soles. He tells me we have to be discreet but he can't help be the center of attention as we walk towards Downtown Cerealand. Towards Sugar Alley.

I've brought it up before, but I haven't really gotten into the sad truths about the pink light district. I'm sure it's exactly what you'd expect from what I've told you about this place already. There are S&M fetish dungeons and live sex shows where the mascots stand in their underwear behind one way mirror so they can't see who's looking at them. All they can see is their sad reflections, forever reminding them of their sad life choices. Or maybe they are all empowered by it and fulfilling their own fetishes. I seriously doubt that's true, though, even if some of them do. The room is small.

There is a stool in it and a sink. A small roll of paper towels and a bottle of Windex. There are shower heads that come out of the ceiling and a drain on the floor. The mascots sit on the stools, looking at themselves in the mirror, waiting to be chosen. When someone chooses them, when they pay the madam at the end of the street, a light comes on in their tiny room. They know they are being watched. Then, depending on what you pay for, things are done to that mascot, or the mascot does things to themselves. But most of the time they are just waiting, staring at themselves in the mirror, waiting.

When we walk by the pink windows I notice a strange person lurking around. Usually, it's couples and lonely perverts who are here, but there's a strange man in a pressed suit with a briefcase. He looks out of place. He is walking by the windows taking in all of his options. He stops in front of a window with Quake in the little room. Quake is an old mascot from a 1970s cereal. It's kind of like Captain Crunch but only a little chalkier. Quake looks like a new kid, fresh out of college. His outfit is just bike shorts and a miner's helmet, the kind with the little light on it. His chin is huge and makes him look like Dudley Do-Right, from the Rocky and Bullwinkle show. He has large blue circles for eyes. I pretend that his backstory is that he had to drop out of college for beating up a pledge at his fraternity. He just got too drunk and went overboard, almost killed this kid. I think it's maybe because he was attracted to this kid and wasn't yet honest with himself enough to accept it, so he channeled it into anger and destroyed this kid's face instead of kissing it. I imagine the kid he beat up's name is Charlie and that before he joined the frat, he wanted to go into medicine. That he didn't even want to join the frat, but his brothers had all been in it and he felt obligated, and now his face is all fucked up and he suffered brain trauma and the kid who beat him up is now a Quake mascot in Cerealand, stripping for strange business men. I name the kid Charlie because I am also thinking of the book, Charlie and the Chocolate Factory. Which is what I used to think working in Cerealand would be like.

The Business Man stops at his window and stares at Quake. Just stares and licks his lips. He turns and nods to an assistant, a small nervous looking woman with thick glasses. I didn't even notice she was there. The assistant nods back and scuttles away. Moments later the light above Quake's window goes out. Which is not usually what happens. Usually, when someone wants a window show, the light turns purple. Then a little curtain gets released so you can get a little privacy. I've never seen the light just go out before. But then again, it might not be that unusual, since I'm not really one to spend money here, for all I know that's just what happens for when you pay for another level of kinky shit. I guess I could ask Sugar Bear about it, he would know since this is technically his part of the park, but he's ahead of me and I don't think he noticed it happening. The Business Man licks his lips again and then heads off away from the window, towards the exit of Sugar Alley. Before I let myself get more invested in this, Sugar Bear takes me down a narrow side street.

I know where he's taking me and why he's taking me there. He probably wants to show me where Sam used to work, which little room was hers. I'm not sure if this is him thinking he is being helpful or just the kind of fucked up thing he thinks is funny, but either way he probably thinks I didn't know. That I haven't been there dozens of times before.

When Sam and I applied to be mascots we had barely done the research to truly understand what we were getting into, what it really meant. The application forms were very long and complicated and Sam didn't feel like spending all her free time reading, when she already knew she wanted to do it. I wasn't like Sam. I needed to be extra sure I understood what we were signing up for. But I also knew that Sam wasn't the kind of girl to wait around or do what someone else told her to do—she was going to apply with or without me, and I knew that if I didn't hurry and catch up to her, I would lose her. I kind of always knew, I guess, that I would lose her eventually no matter what I did. And because I knew this, I also knew I didn't have to do this for her. But I wasn't ready to give her up. So I didn't read the agreement—well, not as thoroughly as I wanted to, and we signed it together.

When the day for our interviews came, Sam was so

excited. She dressed in Tony the Tiger colors and spent all morning doing her hair so the top of her hair looked like it had cartoon tiger ears.

"You're really leaning into this aren't you?" I teased.

"With moments like these, you have to make an impression! You have to let them know you've come to the table with something, and that something better be unique and special—otherwise you'll just be ordinary. And even when you do nothing at all, it takes effort. And who on earth would ever put effort into being ordinary." She crinkled her nose at me and walked through the doors of the corporate offices of Cerealand. I stood outside for a moment. Almost a minute.

I know that what I was thinking at that moment was how in love with her I was, but when I remember this day I like to edit the memory and pretend that in that moment, right after she went inside and before I followed her, that what went through my mind was a gut feeling that this was a bad idea, that I should just walk away and go back to sorting marshmallows. I like to pretend this because it makes my going inside my fault. It makes it so that I did it despite having a premonition that it would all turn out horribly for me. That I forged ahead because *I* wanted it. I don't like thinking that the reason I'm in the hell I'm in is because I loved someone.

The interview waiting room is huge. There are about 20 folding chairs. I notice that they have wheels on them.

I've never seen folding chairs with wheels, and this fascinates me. I try to tell this to Sam but she is already at the window submitting our signed forms. There is no one at the receptionist window, what there is, is an electronic sign in and a small slot where you slide your signed forms through. It's boring and I already am dreading the interview.

On the small triangular table in the middle of this large, quiet and mostly empty, waiting room is a pamphlet with a picture of Captain Crunch on it. It says "So you're joining the family!..." I don't like how there is an ellipsis after the exclamation point. I know ominous isn't the word I'm looking for, but there was something ominous about it. There's nothing else to do so I pick it up to read it. It's brightly colored and inside it there's a little comic where Captain Crunch explains the Mascot interview process. I open the pamphlet but all the words inside are in Hebrew and Japanese. Like both, one on top of the other. Why would they have the cover in English? I try to make sense of the drawings in the little comic but it just looks like nonsense. I look over to show this to Sam, but she's too excited to sit down and is pacing up and down the room. I'm happy we're the only two in here but it also is strange to me that there aren't more people to interview. Or maybe strange is not what I mean, since I don't really care, I just notice that we're the only two there. I just kind of want to get it over with. Very few people get accepted, so maybe with some luck we will get turned down and can go home soon. We aren't really that qualified.

The door opens and a woman comes out holding a clipboard. She is uncomfortably tall and is dressed like BuzzBee the bee from Honey Nut Cheerios. She isn't a Mascot, she's just wearing a striped t-shirt and yellow pants with a stinger sticking out of the butt. She looks ridiculous and I'm not sure what the point of her dressing like this is. I wonder if that's her personal style or if she's forced to dress like that. I guess she could be dressed as a generic bee and not Buzz. I guess there's nothing that distinguishes him from any other bee. The sneakers, maybe?

The very tall woman looks straight ahead and reads our names from the clipboard. She looks around waiting for us to confirm that we are us, despite the fact that we are the only ones here.

"Yes," Sam says. I look over at Sam and realize what I thought was excitement is actually nerves. She is sweating and her palms are cold when I go over to hold them. She pulls her hand away, and I'm not sure if that's because she is annoyed with me or because she is anxious. I'm gonna go with anxious because it means I don't have to figure out which of my annoying habits I need to work on. The woman speaks in a deep voice which reminds me of Nico from the Velvet Underground. I've never heard her voice personally, but my mother would always say that the woman next door sounded like Nico from the Velvet Underground, and the Tall Woman who is dressed like a bee, sounded exactly like our next door neighbor. The voice you would make if you were a trying to suppress a moan of pain while appearing cool and collected. I try to have a wordless exchange with Sam, give her a "this woman is very tall, and also why is she dressed like a bee, and also what's up with her nonchalant-pain-voice, right?" look, but she doesn't see it. She just stands at attention, waiting to be told what to do.

The woman in the bee costume, who I am calling Perla, looks up from her clipboard and speaks to us in a mechanical and disinterested way. It's almost hypnotic and it soothes me, like if someone was giving me a head massage. I decide Perla isn't a good name for her, but I can't think of a better name since her voice is numbing my brain and making it hard to think. She talks for a while, she says things like 'waiver' and 'understand the risks' and something else about 'cost of operation being this and that.' I'm not paying attention and I realize that at some point during this speech I've been taken to a small examining room and Sam isn't there with me. I don't know how I lost track of time this way, but the Bee Woman is still here and now she's talking about something else, she says words like 'randomly assigned' and 'dormitory rules'. I snap myself out of the trance, and focus up. "Wait, what?" I ask.

She looks at me, as if also snapping out of a trance. Seeing me almost for the first time. She gives an annoyed sigh and repeats herself. "If accepted into the program you will be randomly assigned a character to play and will be placed in the appropriate dormitory, where you will be required to obey the dormitory rules."

"Wait, you don't get to choose what mascot you

want to be?" I guess I knew that, it was in the contract and I do remember talking to Sam about it, but it still seemed to catch me off guard. Like I had never heard that this was how they did it. "Do I get to say no if I don't like the mascot they choose?" She stared at me and it felt like she was fighting a lot of discomfort to address me.

"I normally don't get asked so many questions." She says, but in a way that makes it clear she likes how things normally go.

"How do they decide what Mascot I'm going to be?"

She stares me down. It's clear she isn't going to answer me. But I am tired and a little upset that I didn't notice being taken to this little room.

"I think the reason you're not telling me anything," I double down, "is because you don't know shit about what goes on here, do you? You fake ass Bee."

I sit there waiting for something to happen. For her to either react or pretend to ignore it, because I think those are her only options. She looks down at me, making eye contact for the first time and smiles, then she presses a button near the door and walks out locking me in the room with no way out. So she somehow manages to do neither and both. I notice my side of the door has no doorknob. I sit there and look around. There is a small table with that butcher style paper on it that I assume I'm supposed to sit on. I get angry at this whole stupid process, what's with the goddamn mystery? It's all seeming like a pathetic attempt to seem ominous. Yes, now's the time to use that word! I guess it *would* be creepier and more unsettling if they were all cheerful about the whole thing—giving you step by step breakdowns of what was going to happen to you in a sing-song way—but instead, they just leave you waiting. Like an eternal DMV. Very clinical.

There are no magazines in the room, other than the little patient table and a small sink by the door, the room is a blank white, windowless box. I guess it actually is a goods tactic because I am so fucking bored by the time the Bee Woman comes back in with needles and begins to draw my blood, I don't even struggle or ask what's going on because I'm so thankful that something is finally happening. After the blood is drawn I get taken to a machine that takes a full body picture of me. But it's like an x-ray machine that shows not only my bones but all my organs. Someone, a technician I guess, tries to explain to me that what they are doing is scanning my biological makeup to see what characters my body type would be compatible with. I ask if that means I am being accepted, but he tells me that this is standard procedure for all applicants. I ask where Sam is, but he doesn't answer and says "We're all done here" with a stupid smile. He walks out of the room and a nurse walks in and asks me to get into a hospital gown and follow her. The nurse reminds me of the kind of person who was really button up at work, real tight ass, but at home liked getting her feet spanked and tickled as a fetish. I know that people like that exist because movies and cartoon shows have alluded to it, and although I've never seen any foot fetish porn, I have a gut feeling this nurse is really into it. I call the nurse Nurse Pinky in my head. She walks us down a long hallway and the white nurse's shoes click-clack on the floor as if they were tap shoes. We are walking towards a large ornate door where another nurse, this one looks like Kathy Najimy in Sister Act, is standing there with Sam. I guess she also looks like Kathy Najimy in Hocus Pocus. She's like a witch/nun looking nurse. I am so relieved to see Sam, I start to run to her, but Nurse Pinky holds me back and gives me a 'no running in the halls' look. I roll my eyes and start power walking to towards the door.

"Sam! Holy shit, I'm so happy to see you. Are you okay?"

"Hey" she gave me a nervous smile. I reached out for her hand and she took it, gave it a tight squeeze and then let it go. "I'm scared." She said. "Don't be silly, you idiot," I teased, "You're going to do Grrrrrrrrreat." She smiled and crinkled her nose at me. Nurses Pinky and Kathy Najimy rolled their eyes at us and nodded to each other. They opened the big doors and pushed us through.

I'll get into this later, perhaps. But this next part is the part I don't like to talk much about. It's the part of the story that I hate the most. I'm not even sure why, really. I do worse things in this story, way worse. And this wasn't even my fault. I literally had no control over what happened. To her or to me. So I know I shouldn't feel bad about it at all. But I do. So, for now, I'm not going to talk about what happened next with much detail. But the long and short of it was that I got accepted, she didn't and I took the job.

Sugar Bear, it turns out, isn't taking me to Sam's old Pink Light Window, which is all for the best, I guess. Part of me wants to punish myself and make myself stand there. Remember all the things I have tried very hard not to remember or think about. But it's just as punishing to follow Sugar as he leads me to a small window with flickering neon. Inside is an old man who looks like The Cookie Crisp Burglar. He has what appears to be a burglar mask permanently etched on his face, as well as a wispy mustache. He looks like if Hugh Hefner dressed as a cartoon thief for a Halloween Party hosted by someone he didn't care for too much, and so he barely put in the effort. I hope you're picturing it right. This broke ass Hugh Hefner Cookie Crisp Burglar is half asleep when Sugar Bear knocks on his window.

Sugar Bear knows the park better than anyone, and he knows where all the secrets are—well not <u>all</u> the secrets, that was a stupid word to use, more like he knows where a lot of the hidden rooms and passageways are, because he built them himself. This Cookie Crisp sex window is more like the entrance to an old speakeasy. There is a hidden room behind the sleeping Cookie Burglar and Sugar Bear leads me inside. The room is dimly lit and cluttered, but pretty clean despite the stacks of old cereal boxes and discontinued Cerealand merchandise. It looks like a storage closet, but Sugar Bear clears some boxes off what at first I thought was a table but now I realize is a bar. That's when my eyes adjust and I start to see where we actually are. It's a saloon, with a giant stage and a curtain, that I'm sure in its best days, was a bright a vibrant Irish green. There are etchings in the wood, hand carved and incredibly detailed of hearts and horseshoes, clovers and moons. "Where in the fuck are we?" I say, but Sugar Bear ignores me, or finds a very roundabout way of answering the question.

"You see," Sugar Bear has found a box of unopened watermelon whisky bottles and is pouring himself a large glass full. "shit's been going downhill for a long time" Sugar pours whisky into the opened zipper hole that is his snout. "Over the years we've had to shut down lots of rides, restaurants, even Irish Pubs" he gestures around "move them to the back lot of the park, but it's never been like this." He opens another bottle, even though he still has a little less than half left in the first one. I'm half listening because I'm still looking at all the details in this room. It's clearly a Lucky the Leprechaun themed restaurant. Or it was. But it's less an Irish pub and more like an old west saloon. There's the stage and the bar, and even a small piano that's decorated with charms, sitting in the corner. The whole vibe is almost cartoony, but not quite committing to it. "Something rotten is happening Lucky. Mascots are being taken, strange new areas of the park are being used after hours and I'm being kept out of the loop. The missing Toucan is only the tip of the sundae. You're going to have to help me figure out what's been happening to Cerealand."

I looked at him for a long beat. I was exhausted, and the thought of adding more bullshit into the bullshit bucket I was already lugging around was the last thing I wanted. Figuring out what happened to Sam was enough of a pain in the ass without adding a bigger conspiracy to it. Everything about what Sugar Bear was telling me made me tired and want to quit.

I thought about if convincing myself I didn't care about Sam or about any of this would be less stressful and less work than whatever I'd end up having to do with Sugar Bear to '*solve the mystery.*' So while he looked at me, and waited for me to respond, I thought about that.

Sugar had been at the park almost from the beginning. Before he was a bear he was a giant Viking of a man who was the lead engineer and designer of the park. He and Cornelius built the place together. When they figured out that they could genetically change people to make them look more (or less) like cereal mascots, Sugar Bear was one of the first to volunteer for the procedure. He underwent the surgery several times before he became the giant bear he is today. He was basically a giant grizzly with a cartoon bear's face. Sugar was one of the first to embrace the new way of life at the park. Before he went full bear he used to feel like his sex life and work life had to be very separate worlds—but now he was happy. The park was his home, his legacy and his sexual sanctuary. But someone was fucking with it.

"It's not just what happened to the Toucan, there have been lots of mascots disappearing and no one seems to care or notice. And more of those strange new mascots are appearing around the park. The square ones."

"Yeah, I saw them the other day. What are those things?"

"I don't know. I haven't gotten a good look, and I don't want to, baby." Sugar slumped off his stool and sashayed his way toward the bathroom. "If I were you honey," he said, throwing an over the shoulder glance my way, "I'd be thinking of how to bring the whole system down on its cracker ass and piss in its face."

I didn't like being with Sugar Bear for too long. There was something about him that was hypnotic and sick at the same time. Like a lava lamp during turbulence. I didn't have time for conflicting emotions. But I had decided then and there to see this mystery through. I had saved up for a long time and I knew if I wanted to I could (and should) buy myself out of my contract, but I also knew that this poor sap of a bear was all alone, and no one else would believe him, let alone help him. And then of course, there was Sam.

"If you really want to find out what happened to Sam" Sugar said, almost as if reading my mind, "asking for my help is a good place to start. I may seem like a mess, but I love this park, and I'm proud of it, honey"

Sugar winked at me with his large bloodshot eye. He danced his hairy sack of a body towards the bathroom. Humming the sugar crisps theme song as he went.

"Hey Sugar" I called out. He stopped, looked up at me from under the bangs that covered his eyes. The red of the lipstick on his snout shining in the dark room like a cigarette ember.

"It is true you designed all the rides in the park?" I ask him.

"Most of them, yeah."

"Didya design the Lucky Charms ride?"

He smiled. "I did."

"Well fuck you." I lit up a clove. "'Tis a shit ride."

PART TWO

HORSESHOES

I had to get back to work, I couldn't afford another infraction. But something Sugar Bear had told me kept itching at me. How it wasn't just Sam that had gone missing, but how lots of other mascots were just vanishing and how no one seemed to notice or care. When I got back to my Pot of Gold, Dig Em was asleep on his lily pad. At least one thing was the same, no one ever came to this side of the park. I made sure that no one was waiting for me to start the Leprechaun Ride, and I went out behind the tent to smoke and think. I always smoked better when I thought.

I tried to go over the clues in my head one more time. They weren't really clues, just things that may or may not be part of this mystery. The note, the bloody feathers, the Baron, the strange square people, was any of it connected. The note! Sam had written me a note asking me to meet her the day she died. It was still in my work locker back at the employee housing. I figured I should probably go check it out sooner than later. See if there was anything on the note that I missed. But I was tired, and the note wasn't going to go anywhere, and Sam wasn't going to get any more dead. Or missing. But probably dead, right?

I finished my cigarette and asked myself what the fuck was I doing this for.

Years ago, after months of no communication after I took the job as a Cerealand mascot, Sam finally reached out. She had left a note on my locker that asked if I would still recommend her being reconsidered for the Mascot Program. It wasn't a friendly letter, it was very business-like, almost cold. She always wrote in pencil, because she always made spelling mistakes when she wrote, or would sometimes re-think a word and replace it. But she always pushed so hard on the paper, that even though she would erase the words, you could trace your finger over the words she was trying to fix, etched into the paper, and read her mistakes. She had signed the note: *Thanks, Sam.* But it was clear she had started to write something else and then changed her mind writing "Thanks" instead. I felt along the grooves of the paper to try and see if I could make out the word she erased. I was hoping that she was writing *Love*, Sam—but that's not what it was.

Of course, I recommended Sam be re-evaluated. I would have tried to write her back and tell her that it was a horrible job and that it was nothing like what we used to think it would be, nothing like what she kept daydreaming it would be. But I knew that whatever I said wouldn't matter to her. This is what she wanted and I wanted to give it to her. I also thought that if she was finally a Mascot too, she would forgive me, and we would be together again.

"I'm sorry no. We don't do revaluations." Pop said. Snap and Crackle were seated next to her. Shadows cast over their faces, for some reason. They sure loved that conspiracy vibe. "Well, I think you're making a mistake. This applicant really wants the job, she'd be a great addition." I looked at them and for some reason, I am not sure why, I added "I think you get off on choosing people at random. Like it's just as fun rejecting people as it is turning them into freaks." I instantly regretted saying this. But I also had to show resolve, no point in saying something like that and then looking like a scared little bitch. So I stood my ground.

Pop smiled at me. "You have gumption, little Leprechaun. You have courage." She nodded to her sisters who nodded back. "You remind us of someone." She continued "Someone very special. You're like a brave little baby, I just want to put you in my mouth." Her sisters laughed at this.

"That's great," I said. "Well then make a special exception. Reconsider this application."

"We've already told you our decision little baby. If you have nothing else to say, you can leave."

"No. That's not okay." I said. I was pretty small so I couldn't intimidate them the way I wish I could have, if I was say, the Tiger or the Elephant.

"Excuse me?" Pop said, smiling, almost amused at the balls on her little Leprechaun.

"I said bullshit! Well, I said No, that's not okay, but I also call bullshit on this. She and I are a package deal. If you don't approve her, I walk, understand?" An empty threat, I knew it and they knew it. I couldn't leave, I was still very much under contract and I had zero leverage over them.

"I don't understand why you just won't do it? Why the hell do you even care?"

They smile at me, even the sisters in the shadow flash their bright white teeth at me. Taking me in.

"You are quite adorable when you are upset. You have so much fight in you, and that moment, that magical and delicious moment where you will stop fighting and accept your fate will be incredible."

I had no clue what Pop was talking about, I just knew that I had nothing to lose and everything to gain. I looked up at the sisters and prepared a speech I had been practicing in my head since I walked into the judgment chambers.

"I'm going to tell you three a story,—"

"All right, we grant your request."

"Wait," what Pop had said really threw me off my rhythm. "You what?"

"We grant your request, we will reconsider Samantha's application."

"Why?"

"Why what?"

"Why would you just give me what I wanted? You literally were telling me no two seconds ago."

They smiled at each other. It was very unsettling.

"Why do you care? We're giving you what you want. Now scoot my little small one. We have much work to do."

I didn't move. Something was off. Something odd about the whole damn encounter. But I guess I was technically getting what I came for. "Well, that's vague and strange, but fine. I'll take the deal." At that point I just wanted to do right by Sam, and I was still newish to being a mascot, I didn't know how fucked up the Triplets actually were, what they would be capable of. I thought that it was all show, theatrical bullshit to make them feel creepy and powerful.

I wrote a note to Sam that told her I had filled out her application and she had an appointment with the Triplets and slipped it in her locker.

I didn't hear from her again until two weeks later when she left a bright blue feather outside my door.

"But when I got back to the dorms, I saw someone had broken into me locker."

"They stole the note?"

"Yeah. Either that or I didn't leave it in me locker and left it somewhere else. That's also possible."

"What did it say, exactly?"

"That's the thing," I tell Sugar Bear "I don't remember exactly. All I know is that she wanted to meet me at the Crunch Berry tree at 5 pm and she never showed. She stood me up."

"Well, darlin', that's because she was most likely dead."

"Yeah," I say "I guess."

"Did the note say anything else?"

"I'm sure it did. But I don't remember what. I thought the important part was where to meet her and at what time."

"Well, it's important now. What else did you see that night, when you went home?"

"Nothing really," I said, trying to think hard about it, while also trying not to think about anything.

"Although, I remember Trix not being able to sleep because he kept sneezing. He said there was pollen everywhere. Or it could have been the rotten milk from the milk vat."

Sugar Bear gave me a look.

"I know what you're thinking. But it's not the Bee. The Bee is actually more allergic to pollen than Trix. It's something Trix talks about a lot. He thinks it's funny."

Sugar Bear winks at me and places his big bear paw full on my tiny leprechaun ass. He gives it a friendly squeeze, as if telling me it's time to go. Like he knows exactly who we need to talk to next.

"That's not who I was thinking about."

"Me Want Honeycomb!" Crazy Craving shouted as Sugar slammed his back against the wall.

"If you're lying to me, I'm gonna shove my face up your ass."

"Me *want* Honeycomb!" The little monster pleaded with the bear. His little legs kicking the air.

Sugar Bear had taken me to the Honeycomb Hideout to talk to Crazy Cravings. His tiny legs kicking in the air, such a small thing.

"That's bullshit and you know it. Now what the hell were you doing at the Leprechaun's place?" Sugar Bear winked at me, giving me a 'this won't take me long' kind of look.

"Me. Want. Honeycomb." Crazy Craving waved his arms around and snarled at Sugar. His eyes were darting all over the place. Whatever this thing was before he got turned into the Honeycomb Hunger mascot must have been a wild raccoon. I can't imagine a human being was somewhere inside that thing.

"I'm losing my patience with you buddy. You really want Sugar Bear to lose his cool?" Sugar lowered his gaze and stared Crazy Craving right in the eyes. Those big, red, unblinking bear eyes. The monster calmed down, and Sugar Bear smiled.

"Much better, now tell me and my friend, if it's not too much trouble, darlin', what were you doing in this fine gentlemen's room, and did you happen to take a note?"

I had been more focused on seeing Crazy Craving up close than on what Sugar was saying. Because his job was to literally tornado around the park and steal honeycombs from people, I had never seen him up close before, but now I was actually paying attention to what he was. Even this close I still didn't know what the hell he was supposed to be. I guess, from context, he was supposed to be the embodiment of hunger, but up close he looked like a cross between Grizzlor from He-Man and a weasel.

"Me want. Honeycomb. Me want *Honeycomb*—me me want it! Me? Me! Honeycomb big! Not small."

Sugar Bear nodded along, throwing in an occasional "mmhmm" or "okay" as the little monster spilled the beans.

"Me want Honeycomb."

"And that's all you know?"

"Honeycomb!" Crazy Craving scratched at Sugar's arm.

"Okay, okay—you get the fuck out of here before I break your dick!"

I watched as the little guy ran into the night, blurring down the alley like a little tornado.

"He didn't take your note, but he *was* in your room. Probably looking for drugs or something to steal so he can trade it for drugs. That guy really loves drugs." Sugar laughed a little and fished his leather thong out from his ass. He straightened out his baby blue sweater and took out a vail of crushed sugar bear cereal. He did a bump through his snout and roared.

"Come on," Said Sugar Bear "I know where we have to go next."

I was staring out in the direction of the little tornado.

"I'd never met that guy before," I said. "All he can say is 'Me want Honeycomb'?"

"What? No—he can talk fine. He's just an asshole."

Sugar Bear and I head down to watch the main street parade. He doesn't tell me where we are going or who we are looking for, which annoys me because this was really my investigation and it's really my ex-girlfriend who went missing. But I also have no idea what I would be doing without his help so I just let him lead. Sugar is telling me a story about how when he started building the rides he assumed they would be primarily for kids. Most of his rides were modeled after the Disney story rides at Disneyland, where you just sat in a car while it took you through miniature sets and puppets that reenacted your favorite animated movies. Cerealand was supposed to do that but with commercials. You were supposed to feel like you were one of the kids in these old cereal ads where you'd interact with a cartoon character and stuff yourself silly with sugar. Over time, people stopped caring about that. And most of the rides were closed down. He's telling me something about how the monster castle he was designing was really scary, for kids anyway. "We had a lab for Dr. Frankenberry and a castle for Count Chocula. It was going to be really great. But when Cornelius died those three bitch daughters of him shut the whole project down. Killed my babies. So I just said to hell with it, if what these bitches want is hedonism that's part of a complete breakfast, then that's what I'll fucking give em!"

The parade was about to start. Normally I would have to be a part of it, as a mascot you were supposed to cycle through and do the parade once a week. But I'd been thankfully overlooked, maybe because I was too small, or didn't really perform the way the other mascots did, and so I hadn't been asked to participate in over a month. I swear if I wasn't under contract and they hadn't spent the money transforming me into Lucky the Leprechaun, I would have been fired a long time ago. The parade is late, and the crowd is getting restless just waiting around on the street. Sugar Bear shrugs and makes his way to a Cotton Candy stand, he orders two large Cottons with cocoa pebbles and cinnamon toast crunch dust sprinkled on top. Even though he looks like a bear, he is still a human being, and I don't think he realizes what that much sugar is going to do to him. Or maybe he does. Maybe he's smarter than I think he is and he's just trying to eat enough sugar to kill himself.

The Parade finally starts. Normally it would be Pop, or one of her sisters, that announces the evening parade. But tonight there is no announcement. The parade just unceremoniously starts up, with the generic marching music announcing the parade floats as they slowly make their way down the main strip of the park. The cars are big and square, all made to look like giant breakfast tables. The kind you would always see in the commercial, with a nice checkered tablecloth, a pitcher of Organic OJ and a small plate with two pieces of almost burnt toast. In the middle of the table, dancing around and waving to the crowds were the Cereal Mascots.

Immediately we see that all the normal mascots are gone. All the usual suspects, Tony the Tiger, Sonny the Cocoa Puffs Bird, Buzzbee the Honey Nut Cheerios Bee, Melvin the Mexican Cocoa Krispie Elephant, aren't there.

I do see Dig Em and Trix and wave to them, but they don't see me or are too busy prancing around the fake breakfast table to wave back. I also notice a whole bunch of random characters—I can recognize some them from pictures of their cereal boxes that my mom used to have around the house, but I've never seen them in the park before— they must be new recruits. But why would they make these old broke-ass characters instead of making more Frosted Flake Tigers or Corn Flake Roosters?

"What in the world are these things supposed to be?" Sugar Bear asks me, with a mouth full of cotton candy. I notice he is standing next to me again.

"Well," I say and start to scan the floats. "there's The Vitamin King, and I think that purple thing is supposed to be the Quisp alien, and that's the Fruity Yummy Mummy." I notice someone else on the float. He kind of looks like a Red version of Grapefellow. And then it hits me, Baron Von Redberry. Grapefellow's old cartoon nemesis. *The Baron.* Was that what Grapefellow was talking about? And now that I think of it, why isn't Grapefellow in the parade?

"No, idiot. I know who the mummy is, and the alien. I mean those things." Sugar Bear snaps me out of my daydream and back to the matter at hand. And that's when I see what he's talking about. A float with some of those strange square mascots on it. They are still far enough away that we can't see the detail in what they are, but the closest I can tell is that they are supposed to be, I don't know, Mini Wheats. I say as much to Sugar Bear.

"As far as I can tell, and I can't get a good look from way over here, but they look like Mini Wheats to me."

"They don't look frosted. I don't think they are mini wheats."

"They make unfrosted mini wheats," I say.

"No they don't."

"Of course they do. Why would they emphasize frosted if they didn't have a non-frosted option."

"What? I don't follow that logic."

"What I mean is,—"

"That doesn't matter, what matters is that only Frosted Mini-Wheats ever had a cartoon mascot and those square whatever the fuck they are's—don't look frosted to me."

"So?" I say.

"So I don't think they are supposed to be Mini Wheats."

"Well what do *you* think they are?" I challenge.

"Whatever they are," he says quietly, "they're gone."

I look up and he's right. The parade is over and the floats are long gone.

"Let's get something to eat." Says Sugar Bear stuffing the last of the cotton candy into the zipperflap of his leather gimp mask. "There's nothing much for us to do for now."

I don't think that's true, we have several leads to follow. And Sugar Bear said he knew who we had to talk to next, but all we did was watch the parade. We're no closer to understanding anything. And as far as I can tell we have no plan. But I realize I haven't eaten all day, and it's getting dark and I probably should force something down my throat so I can keep going. "Okay," I said, "Let's get something to eat."

"What are you in the mood for?" He asks, batting his long fake eyelashes at me, somehow, through the eyeholes in his mask.

"Anything but cereal."

On our way to the cafeteria we see businessmen all over the park. They are all wearing very nice suits that Sugar Bear can place (designer, cut, year) and he knows these men don't belong here. What would, obviously very rich and stylish, business men be doing at the park? And where is everyone else? Normally the park, even on its slowest day, would have some crowd at the strip club or the cereal bar. But the place looks like it was closed for a convention of blank-eyed businessmen.

I see another one of those square mascots. I'm tired of not knowing what the fuck they are so I walk towards one, it doesn't seem like they can move fast at all, but I'm having trouble catching up to them. I'm so distracted that I don't see myself bump into a Japanese businessman with a briefcase.

"Oh, excuse me. I was—I'm sorry." I look at him, and he just stares at me. He licks his lips and moves on.

I watch him walk away, he's heading towards the back part of the park, where the closed rides are.

"Should we follow him?" I ask Sugar Bear, but when I look around to see where he is, I can't find him. I'm in the middle of Main Street and all I can see are businessmen in perfectly ironed suits, carrying briefcases. It takes me a moment to realize they are all staring at me. They are standing perfectly still and all lick their lips in unison. I realize that the smart move here would be to not wait around and figure out what's going on, and even though it attracts more attention on me, I've seen enough movies to know that you don't hesitate in moments like these, that you don't stick around to make sure if you're actually in danger or if you're being paranoid. So I run, I run as fast as my tiny legs can run.

When I get back to the dormitory I see Trix is in our room. I've never been so happy to see the stupid Rabbit before.

"Trix, holy shit—where ya outside just now?"

Trix looks at me and frowns

"You shouldn't be swearing, it's against the rules. Plus you should be packing up your stuff, you don't live here anymore."

"Yeah, well fuck that. There's something very strange happening here."

"Yeah I know, your girlfriend's dead, or missing, probably dead. Ex-Girlfriend. That's not a good reason to curse. Also, death is a part of life. I've already begun training new potential mascots. More people are signing up, and we'll soon have all sorts of new blood around!"

"Why would anyone want to work here with all the fucked up shit that's happening!?"

"Lucky! Please, the language! Besides, you're over-reacting as usual. Lots of people would still be proud to be a mascot. Cerealand is still a magical place."

"Jesus Trix, haven't you noticed the strange things happening? Haven't you noticed how no one really cares that more and more people are disappearing? I don't know what happened to Sam, and now Sugar Bear is missing. Don't you care that the park is full of strange new Square Mascots and foreign businessmen? None of this bothers you!?"

"Not really. We live in an amusement park for adults, Lucky. When everything is strange, that probably means everything is normal."

"Something is happening and I'm finding out what it is."

"That's cool," Trix says getting into bed and turning out the light.

"Are you going to find out what it is right this moment?"

I just stare at him and don't answer.

"Well then, you can sleep for now and solve it tomorrow. Along with where you're moving to. You can stay here one more night, but I'm serious, I need you out of here by tomorrow. Good night Lucky." The rabbit covers his head under the sheets and does this stupid fake snoring sound he does before he actually falls asleep. I've asked him not to do this, but he does it anyway.

⊍

The next morning I get up right away and I go back to the Cereal Bar to look for Sugar Bear—but when I get there the place is closed. I look around and see a few tourists waiting in line for the Honeycomb Hayride, but not much else. There are no businessmen in well-ironed suits, no assistants following them around. It looks like a normal afternoon, and I wonder if I'm going crazy. I wonder, even though I'm sure that this isn't it, if in my desperation to find something sinister I just let my imagination get the better of me. That it didn't make any sense for two dozen businessmen to have looked at me as if they were about to eat me alive. But I know what I saw. And even though I don't believe my memory of what happened to me at all, because it sounds so stupid and unlikely, I still know that it must have happened.

I decide to look for Sugar Bear near the entrance of the park. I'm walking towards the front gate when a tiny car, like a fancy clown car or a tricked out power wheel, aggressively hits its breaks in front of me. The windows of this tiny car are tinted, and I imagine there is a tiny gangster inside the car, with a tiny driver. I imagine the tiny gangster's name is Sunmi and she is from a Korean gang. When she was three years old, I tell myself, she saw her sister get murdered in front of her by a group of drunks. They beat her to death with a pool cue outside of an arcade. I don't know how that is directly connected to how she became a high profile gang boss, but I imagine this fueled a deep rage as a foundation to her character, and that even though she is obviously tiny, because in my mind she is still a small child, she has risen to the highest ranks of the crime syndicate based on her ability to be sociopathically ruthless while still being adorable. By the time I notice the tiny car doors have opened, it's too late to be disappointed by the fact that it's just BuzzBee and not a tiny Korean gangster. He nods at me, making that 'Get In' gesture with his head. But I just look at him. There's no way I'm getting in that asshole's car.

"There's no way I'm getting in your car, asshole," I say.

"Lucky! Come on, this is serious. I know you've been trying to figure out what's been going on. We need to talk."

"Then come outside and talk to me in the open. I'm not getting in yer wee little clown car."

"It's not safe here." He whispers. I look around. It's quiet and boring and I can't imagine a safer place to have a private conversation.

"You have to drive me around the park then, help me look for Sugar Bear," I ask.

"Fine," he says, "just get in." He buzzes.

Inside Buzzbee's tiny car I realize that there is no driver and that Buzz is controlling it with a little remote control. I don't think I've really ever gotten used to how small I am, and because of that I push that fact out of my mind. I don't feel like a tiny cartoon leprechaun and so I always forget I am one. But it's hard to ignore how tiny you are when you are comfortably sitting in a modified half golf cart that wouldn't be able to accommodate two St. Bernards. This makes me think about movie Beethoven. The one about the giant St. Bernard. Normally this is when I would look up and realize that the person I was with had been talking this whole time, but Buzz was just staring at me. He had sniffing tobacco on his gloved left wrist and would periodically take a sniff. I stared at him staring at me, and it reminded me of the dream I had, where I kept looking at myself sleeping on the train. Buzz, without breaking eye contact, reached into a little pocket and pulled out a small metal tin. He softly poured more of the fine tobacco powder onto his glove, forming a little hill, and just let it sit there. Then he put the tin away and blinked. Not knowing what else to do to break the silence without speaking first, I softly blew at the mound of snuff, blew it right into the Bee's eyes.

"Goddamn it Lucky!" He rubbed his eyes.

"What the hell 'tis this all about Bee? You ask me to get in and you just stare at me like some sort of retarded mannequin!"

"Ow, you're shouldn't use that word." His eyes were watering.

"Start talking or start driving me around the park so I can find the bear, but one of those things better happen now. I'm so tired of all this running around in circles bullshit."

Buzzbee's eyes blinked out the last of the dust, and he gave me 'fuck you' look. Not a sexy fuck you but an angry fuck you. I want to make that clear.

He sighed and picked up the remote control from the floor of the car and started driving us around the park.

"You know, Lucky, I have many a friend in Cerealand, but somehow, just because you despise me, you are the only one I trust."

"That's Peter Lorre." I say.

"What?"

"You're quoting Peter Lorre from that movie."

"No I'm not."

"Yes. Casablanca. That's the line from it."

"I don't know what you're talking about." Says the Bee.

"Fine. I'm all for keeping this conversation going but I want you to know that I know what you just did, and I don't want you thinking you got away with anything." I give him a nod, as if I just told a good joke. Because I want him to know I'm relaxed.

"Whatever. Listen, there are treats in the dark for those of us daring enough to trick, eh?"

I frown at him.

"Now you're just being fucking strange for the sake of it."

"What? I'm talking small. They like the *small* ones." His eyes are big and wide, almost frightened—as if Bee's wide cartoon eyes could show any emotion other than annoyance and joy—but he seemed panicked. "Small ones survive the longest. Large ones, valuable to others. Dry lips."

"What the fuck are you talking about? Bee, you're seriously making it very hard to not kick you right in the taint."

"Grapefellow knew. Now he is gone. He was not small."

"What? What happened to Grapes?"

"Snapped, not even good enough for dry lips."

"You're all over the map here, Bee. Let's take this one step at a time. One, what the fuck are you talking about? Two, what happened to Grapefellow? Three, what do you mean by Dry Lips and Small Ones? Maybe that one should be two, and Grapefellow should be three."

"What?" The Bee looked at me, confused.

"Never mind. What about Toucan Sam, have you heard anything about what happened to her?"

Bee stopped the little car and looked up at me, "I'm sorry Lucky. I'm pretty sure she wasn't small."

"Pretty sure? I need a pretty sure the way I need a thumbtack in my dick. What can you tell me that isn't a fucking riddle?" I grabbed the Bee by his little stinger and clasped my fist tight.

"I heard," I started, while digging my finger into the fleshy part at the base of his stinger, "that when a bee stings you its intestines get pulled out of its asshole. And it dies a painful death."

"That's not really how it works exactly." The Bee said.

I yank at the stinger and Buzz's eye grow wide.

"Then let's find out how it works, exactly."

I pull again, this time not letting myself show restraint so the Bee knows I mean business.

"Holy shit Lucky, stop! Okay. Okay." He shrieks. But I keep going. Having fun for the first time in days.

"Have you ever seen the Dreamworks movie, Bee Movie?"

"Lucky, let go!" He tries to swat at me but I flick him in the face with my free hand and this dazes him.

"It's a Jerry Seinfeld movie, about cartoons bees and how they sue Ray Liotta, the actor, for selling honey without their permission. I mean it's slightly more complicated than that, the Bee starts dating a human woman voiced by Renée Zellweger. I mean this tiny Bee is actually going on dates with a human woman and suing an actor over honey profits! Oh and the bee puns! So many terrible bee puns!"

"Why are you telling me this?" The Bee whimpers as I twist his stinger like a dagger, deeper into his guts.

"I'm telling you this because I've never hated anything to do with Bee's more than Bee movie, until this conversation."

He nods to me.

I ease up on the stinger but I don't let it go.

"All I know is that mascots have been disappearing Lucky, first it was hard to notice. There were so many of us and we are all over the park—it made sense that you could go weeks without seeing a specific mascot. But when Tony went missing, well that was noticeable. Not long after I started suspecting that there was a connection between the disappearances and these strange new mascots I would see around the park." The Bee is breathing heavy.

"The square things?"

"Exactly. I am not sure what they are but I know that the Soggies are in charge of them and of keeping them hidden. I've tried to follow them or find out more but I keep hitting dead ends."

I realize that there is not much more BuzzBee can tell me. And most of what he's told me I already know so he's been pretty much useless. However what he said gives me an idea.

"Okay. Listen, drop me off. I got to go do something."

"Lucky, listen, if we work together—"

I cut him off because I don't want to hear it.

"Shut up Bee, I'm going to figure out what happened to Sam. And then I am going to buy my way out of my contract and get the fuck out of here and never have to look at your gross deformed Bee face ever again." I then add "Because you're gross and you gross me out."

The Bee pulls the car over. He brings it to a soft stop and I open the door to get out. He looks up at me.

"I wish you luck getting out of here, but my friend, let me be frank, it would take a miracle to get you out of Cerealand, and the Krispies have outlawed miracles."

"That's also a Peter Lorre quote, you dumb fuck. Also from Casablanca." I say to him.

But as I get out of the car I know that he's right and that in the end it will indeed take a miracle to get out of here.

The Bee drops me off where he picked me up. It's like we just rode around in a circle around the entrance and it reminds me that everything we do in life is pointless. That we're all just waiting around to die. I wonder what life would have been like if I was born into a family of sailors. If I was raised on a boat and learned to swim with dolphins. I wonder if I would have drowned by now. Even the best swimmers drown, and I've heard that dolphins have been known to roam the open waters, looking for things to sexually assault. I'm not joking. They will pull a grown human underwater with their penis. You see, dolphins have a prehensile penis, made up of powerful muscles, and they can wrap it around objects, such as a human wrist, ankle, neck, or waist—whatever they can grab, really. And it's that tight grip, like a boa constrictor or an elephant's trunk, that drags you down to an underwater cave where you are repeatedly raped and torn apart by the dolphins. To be fair to these Dolphins, they have been known to do this with mannequins more than with actual people. Which I guess is okay. Unless you believe, like I do, that mannequins feel shame.

The park looks deserted and because it's winter the sun is setting at 4 pm. It's dusk and the entrance to Cerealand looks peaceful to me for the first time in so long. It's quiet and still. But then it hits me, why is it so quiet and still? I notice the nervous girl walking around the Milk Fountains. The girl from last night who was at the Pink Windows with one of the businessmen. I get closer to her, and I see she is furiously writing things down in a little notepad, she looks up and around her, like a squirrel, and then begins to scurry off. I decide I *have* to find out what she's doing, because I have nothing else to go on and I don't want to go back to work.

She walks down a narrow walkway, that seemingly leads to a staff entrance for maintenance and up a small street I've never noticed before. It's behind the many gift shops by the entrance and unless you knew to look you'd never find it hidden behind some crunchberry bushes. I can't see her, she's too far ahead of me, but I can hear her little fast paced footsteps on the fruity-pebble- cobblestoned street. We get to a little clearing and I hide behind a lamppost as I watch her scuttle her way towards what looks like a secret bar. It's small but I can hear lots of voices and music coming from inside it. I notice a small neon sign that flashes on and off, "Grins & Smiles & Giggles & Laughs." Must be the name of the bar. It's not curious to me that I've never seen this, because like we've covered, I don't get out much. But it's strange that it's so off the beaten path, so hidden away. I can see the entrance and when the little assistant woman opens the door but the quick peek I get of the inside tells me nothing. Fuck it, I think, I've come this far and I've got nothing else to go on, it's a good a lead as any to see if I can information out of that little nervous woman.

I walk towards the bar, I'm not sure why I'm so nervous about it. Maybe I'm just hopeful that this is a place where I finally get some answers. This woman has to know what's up with all the businessmen being here and I am sure that's somehow connected to the missing mascots. I am feeling a little bolder, now that I have some kind of plan, some agenda. I walk up to the door but before I can open it, two giant hands reach down and toss me into the trees. I fly through the air, branches hitting my face like hard wooden fingers hitting a bongo drum, and for a moment—I'm free.

When I came to, I saw Sugar Bear's fishnet stocking and leather boots hovering over my face. I looked up and took in the rest of him.

"Good you're awake." He said.

I got up slowly and checked my pockets.

"Lucky, you should be happy I was here when I was. You were about to walk into the Grins & Smiles & Giggles & Laughs. That's a Soggie Only bar—and *that's* where they've been taking the mascots—the strange ones. There's something really bad going on in there, and you'd be feeding yourself to the lion's den's mouth if you had walked in there."

"I can't find my cigarettes," I said.

"Goddamn it are you listening to me?"

"Yes! But I am stressed out right now and would really like to smoke."

I took in a deep breath. We were out by a lot of trees, so the air was clear and rich with oxygen and I wasn't used to it. I coughed and calmed down.

"I guess I should thank you for 'saving' me."

"What's with the tone? I *did* save you."

"Well how do you know so much about this? And you just happen to be here when I'm about to open the door. Too obvious. Seems like you're the perfect person to be playing both sides and priming me for a down and dirty double-cross. And no one plays Lucky like a bitch." I looked up at him, seeing if he would flinch. I got nothing. I can't help thinking the speech I gave would have looked cooler if I had been smoking.

"You're an idiot." He said and knelt down so he could be closer to my eye level. "I know this seems like this is all happening at once, but to me this is a long journey I've been on. It's been hard to pretend to be oblivious while trying to get information, figure things out. And it's been harder to keep myself safe—what with everyone vanishing. For some reason, smaller characters are being spared, and so I need someone like you, someone who they aren't focusing on, to help me. We need to get into that bar, but only Soggies can make it through those doors without calling way too much attention to themselves. So I need someone inconspicuous to go in posing as a Soggie."

His big eyes were moist. I'm not sure if that's because he was emotional over being so vulnerable with me, or because he was probably high on any number of things, but I bought into it.

"Okay then Bear, what do we do?"

"Well I have an idea, but I don't think you're going to like it."

Remember when I told you Soggies looked like living puddles of milky semen? If I didn't, or if I didn't put it exactly that way, then I meant to, because that's exactly what they look like. Like melting wax sculptures covered in cum. To masquerade as one of them, to find the right consistency for the costume, would be hard to do with everyday materials from the arts and crafts store, however, as Sugar Bear suggested, there was another way you could go about looking like a Soggie.

"Don't miss," I said.

"I'm not going to miss, and please shut up—it breaks my concentration."

"I'm sorry," I said. "Just please warn me when you're about to finish so I can close my eyes and mouth."

"Please shut up."

Sugar Bear had his eyes closed and was stroking furiously. Nothing was happening.

"Maybe if you go slow and then fast, you know alternating,"

"I know how to jack myself off!" He kept going but it was obvious that he was dropping to half-mast.

"Your dick's going soft man."

"I know what my dick's doing! Just please be quiet."

"Is there something you want me to say? You know, that might help? Like role-play or something?"

He opened his eyes and looked at me. He snarled and growled, baring his teeth and ripping the corners of his leather gimp mask. I jumped back, genuinely terrified.

Sugar Bear smiled. "Oh shit, make that face again."

"What face?"

"That face you just made. When you thought I was going to eat you."

"I never thought you were going to eat me."

"Whatever, that face, you made this amazing, terrified face. Do that again."

"I don't know if I can fake it."

"Try. Please, it's the only way I think I'm gonna get off."

I tried making faces and pretending to be scared but it didn't work. Sugar tried attacking me again, but I kept seeing it coming and I still couldn't give him what he wanted. If I was going to be able to get into that bar and get the next puzzle piece we needed, I had to find a way to get Sugar Bear to ejaculate all over me. I had to tap into something real to trigger me, so I thought back to the most terrified I've ever been.

I think back to my operation. When I first became a mascot. Sam had left the building in tears and I was immediately taken to an operating room. They used anesthetic but it wasn't normal numbness but a strange feeling that left me semi-conscious. I didn't drift away like the time they took my tonsils out when I was eight years old and they told me to count backwards from ten. I remember that feeling like the world went black, feeling like I was a marble, spiraling around a black sink until I sank away down the drain. But this was different. I was aware of where I was, and what was happening to me, only I couldn't move. I could still feel my body, sort of. I could feel them injecting me with thick needles and the sharp, freezing pain of something being shoved into my bloodstream. I wasn't numb—not in the normal sense—it was as if my skin was a coat, a thick heavy coat and I just wanted it off my body. It itched, my skin felt like it wasn't part of me, I felt the veins and muscles suffocating under it, I wanted to tear it off, but I couldn't move.

"What's wrong with him?" I heard someone walk into the room and stand over me. My vision was watered down because tears had formed on my eyes. I couldn't blink the water out to get a clean look but I could tell it was Pop. "I guess he's reacting strangely to the anesthetic." Crackle, I think, shrugged as if this wasn't her problem. She was eager to start. My eyes were still open, still full of water but I could see the blurry unmistakable shape of one of the Triplets flip a switch and I hear the whir of machinery. My eyeballs are hard to move, my whole body feels like it's made of dry leaves. Like if I were able to move, my skin will crumble right off of me. My eyes try to dart around my head but I can't see anything except operating lights. The bright lights and the strange feeling of being paralyzed makes my heart beat loudly in my ears. My face is red hot, it feels like my eyes are going to melt. My spine feels brittle, like a hollow branch about to snap. I want this to stop but I can't move. I can see someone out of the corner of my eyes, grabbing something from a metal counter.

"Now sisters," Pop says, "what shall we turn this one into?"

The operation lasts hours. At some point, I put it together that I'm being turned into the Lucky Charms Leprechaun. The process isn't cosmetic, it's genetic. I am not sure what they have injected me with, but it's turned my body into a moldable clay. My eyes are now puddles and I can't make out anything, but I can feel three sets of hands moving me around. Scrapping at my face and body. I am sure that I am going to die, that this was all a huge mistake and I am just getting murdered. But then something is placed in my mouth. It's warm and the moment I wrap my lips around it fills my mouth with sweet hot liquid. It tastes like frosted flakes sugar milk and I inhale it down my throat. The more I drink the more the world comes back into focus, the more my body becomes solid and I can move it again. I look up and see Pop, she is breastfeeding me. I'm too hungry to stop or care, I smile as I drink. Never thinking I'll be able to have enough. Ready to suck her dry. But eventually, I stop. I am full and tired and my body aches. The unclear shapes of Crackle and Snap lift me up and parade me around the room. I am too weak to do anything but let them. I can barely keep my eyes open. It takes all the energy I have to lift my head up for a moment. I try to get a good look around the room and notice that there are people sitting in chairs around the table. I hadn't noticed them before. I try to get a better look at them as I am being wheeled out of the operating room, but there is hardly any light, although I could have sworn they were all wearing Captain Crunch masks. Plastic ones. Like the old Halloween masks that would cut into the side of your face like a dull blade.

When I found out that I had been turned into the

Leprechaun I didn't think it would be this terrible. As I remembered him, Lucky was basically just a human looking cartoon character that dressed in a green suit with a dumb green bowler hat. Other than a few cartoony features, Lucky was basically a human. I didn't think it would be that huge of a deal.

"What the fuck happened to me?" I was looking at myself in a small hand mirror.

"I don't look anything like Lucky the Leprechaun!" I said. My ears were long and pointy, like flesh triangles stuck to the side of my face. My eyes were two pink dots barely surrounded by a circle of white. My nose was just two small nostrils on an upturned little pig snout, and my jaw looked drawn on. The worst was what seemed like permanent blushing cheeks tattooed on my face. I looked like the kind of old creepy doll a Grandmother would have made for you if she thought you were a dick and wanted to scare you.

"Pretty sweet huh?" I turned and saw someone who had apparently been in the same recovery room as I was this entire time and I hadn't noticed. He had been turned into Sonny the Cocoa Puffs bird. He had fuzzy small feathers all over his body that looked more like shag carpet than feathers. His nose and jaw had been extended to give him the appearance of a large, pelican-like beak.

"How are they going to change us back though?" I asked him.

"What do you mean?" He said, half listening to me, already practicing his *Coocoo for Coco Puffs* line.

"I mean when we don't want to work here anymore,

they're supposed to change us back!"

"Yeah, I don't see that happening. I mean this looks pretty permanent." He is touching his grotesque beak face, running his fingers over his fuzzy fur feathers. He is loving this.

"But they said they would change us back, it's in our contracts, isn't it!?" I am panicking now.

"I don't know." Sonny went back to looking in the mirror and practicing his catchphrase.

I start crying so hard that I can't breathe.

"Don't do that." He says.

I had teared up at my own memories when I felt the fire-hose-like strength of Sugar Bear's powerful stream of sperm. It was like getting sprayed by a warm fire extinguisher. A fire extinguisher! That also would have worked! The stench of it was overwhelming. It felt thick and suffocating, but also fluid and alive as if I could feel the billions of sperm cells wiggling and tickling me. It was like being covered in a wet beach blanket, but also being massaged by infinite, tiny slimy ants. The smell was like old soap and even older milk, with a subtle scent of golden crisps. I wondered for the first time, if that was because he was a bear who ate honey or if it was part of the character. That his cum would taste like his cereal. I wondered if my semen tasted like Lucky Charms.

I stood there and tried to see through the milky costume that covered me.

"How do I look?"

"Better lose the hat," Sugar said.

"Okay, I'm going in I guess." I started to slosh my way towards the door. "Oh, what should I be looking for, or asking about?"

"How should I know?" Sugar Bear was annoyed when he said this, though I think he had no reason to be. Instead of getting into a whole thing with him about how this was all his fucking idea to begin with, I decided to just wing it, because I wanted to get it over with and wash this bear's semen off of my body. A thought I pray I only ever have to think once.

I walked inside the bar. Tables full of off-duty Soggie officers looked up at me. I planned on just walking in, like I was used to this place, and not draw too much attention to myself, but instead I froze and looked up at everyone staring at me. Meeting each individual pair of eyes. What was probably two seconds passed by like minutes. Until a large gloop of my costume plopped onto the floor with a loud, *glumpsh*. I turned to see if anyone was looking at the consistency of the gloop on the floor, knowing that Soggies don't gloop like that, and ready to fight my way through this bar. They didn't have a pool table, which sucked, because the fight I was preparing to have was relying on me being able to use a pool cue as a weapon, but that's when I noticed they weren't looking at me, but at a TV monitor above the door that was showing an old sports game.

I walked up to the bar and ordered a cold spiced milk, unsure of what my next move was going to be.

I looked around the bar, barely taking in the decor, as I scanned the room, Where's Waldo style, for the assistant I had followed here.

I see her. She is sitting at a table with two Soggies. The same two Soggies I had seen before, with the melting mascot. They are trying to make conversation with her, but she's trying as best she can to look busy and write in her notebook so she doesn't have to talk to them much. At least that's what I assume, based on the body language I take in from across the room. I decide I'm going to walk over and talk to her, but I should come up with something interesting to say, since it's clear that she isn't here to talk. Why is she here? She's the only non-Soggie (besides me, I guess) in the bar. It has to mean something.

I get closer to the table, being careful not to make it obvious that I'm trying to eavesdrop. But before I can focus on what the people at her table are talking about I get distracted by the word eavesdrop. What a strange word. I mean if I was told to come up with a word that meant secretly listening in on someone else's conversation, eaves-drop is not what I would come up with. What a stupid fucking word. Oh yeah, words. I go back to trying to hear what is being said at the table, with the strange assistant and the two Soggie officers. It's loud and crowded and there are a lot of echoes in this strange little bar, but I am able to make out what she is saying. Sort of. I stare at her mouth, trying to see if I can read her lips—but I have a lot of jizz in my eyes, so everything is kind of blurry. I get closer. I hear her talking to one of the Soggies, this one is not wearing a hat. She is saying something like "I don't care what happened. My boss already paid and he' doesn't care that it was an accident."

The Soggie is looking at her without listening to her. Just staring at her. Smiling.

The other Soggie, this one *is* wearing a hat, speaks up.

"Listen, we are sorry. We already have spoken to the team at the Lab, and the Triplets are going to make someone new for your boss. Someone special."

"He doesn't want *someone special,* he paid for the Tiger."

"Listen lady, at the end of the day, can you really even tell who the hell is in there? He'll be happy, trust me."

The assistant looks to other Soggie, to see if he has anything to add. He just smiles at her, sheepishly.

"He better be, or it's my ass. And if it's my ass, then I'm coming for yours. Both of you."

She gets up and walks to the bathroom.

The two Soggies sit there and make sure she is out of earshot before they start to talk.

"She's never going to go for it." Said the Soggie, the one with the hat on.

"Why the fuck not? I think we're hitting it off. It's not out of the realm of possibility." Said the other Soggie, who didn't have a hat.

"Because," said Hat Soggie "Humans don't want date living piles of milk who work as security guards at a third-rate amusement park."

"She's not like that. She's very smart, and she's above all of that shit. Plus I don't think she wants to work for that creep she's working for, I think I could talk her into coming to work here." Said Hatless Soggie.

"And what, become a fucking mascot?"

"No way! She's seen firsthand what happens to them. I was thinking something more administrative. Head office kind of gig. I think if I can help make that happen, I could be in a better position to ask her out."

"Dude, that's crazy. She's here now, just make your move, get rejected and move on so I don't have to hear you talk about this shit anymore."

For some reason I spoke up, I didn't realize I was saying this out loud, I guess I was just going to sound it out in my head, test out how it played, see if it was worth saying out loud, but I guess I didn't switch to inner monologue because I looked right at them and said,

"I know her. I could talk to her if you'd like. I know she likes you, she's just intimidated is all."

The two Soggies looked at me. They could tell something about me was off. Also, I could feel the Sugar Bear semen start to harden, and look less Soggie-like by the second.

"Who the fuck are you?" Said Hat Soggie.

"I'm the guy who can help you score that tasty dame in the toilet over there. Just let me talk to her."

"And why would you do that?" Hatless Soggie said.

"Because I want to do Lab or whatever, I want to go to the Lab and work at that place." I was barely able to speak. Words stumbling out of my mouth like half-chewed thoughts.

"You want to get moved to Lab duty?" They said, confused.

"Yes, sure. That's what I mean. Lab duty."

"You want us to get you on Lab duty, and then you'll talk to the assistant, whom you know, and get her to date me?" Hatless sounded very dubious as he said this out loud. I lifted my arm to try to give him a reassuring thumbs up, but I noticed my costume was drying quickly and was cracking. Shit, I have to get out of here.

"Listen, just let me do the next lab whatever and you can get to know her better. I'll send over a pitcher for your table."

They looked at me, I could tell that, like me, the idea of not having to work and just drink or hang out was a good offer. A gift horse. So they looked at each other and nodded.

"Fine, but don't fuck this up. We already melted one of those things by accident and now the Krispies are all mad at us."

"Don't worry. I'll do a good job. Where's the lab again?"

They looked at me, squinting their eyeless eyes.

"Where did you say you worked again?" Said Hat Soggie.

"I'm new."

"That's not what I asked."

I take a total shot in the dark.

"The Baron sent me."

This stops them. They look at each other, and share a tense look. I'm not sure if they recognize the name or have no idea what I'm talking about. Then they look at me right in the eyes. I remember that Soggies don't have pupils. And they were staring right at my eye dots. They knew, I knew they knew, or at least would know very soon.

"What's wrong with your eyes?" Hatless said.

"I have pink eye. It's gross." I lied.

They looked at me, not buying it. I noticed the table next to us had a bottle of hard liquor, 100 proof vodka, and they were messily pouring shots. Spilling the booze all over the table and floor.

I kicked the table and the bottle rocked off the surface and crashed at our feet. I fished out my lighter, flicked it on and let it drop to the floor.

Sugar Bear at first keeps an eye on the door after I walk inside. Making sure I don't get tossed out or call for help. But nothing happens and Sugar gets tired of just staring at the door. He begins to look around the bar, getting a little closer, and notices that the windows outside the small wooden building have been boarded up from the inside and you can't peek at what's going on in the bar. Which is a little creepy but not that odd. Sugar then walks to the back of the building. There's a small dumpster with a lock on it, and what looks like the hatch to a bomb shelter sticking out of the ground. It reminds him of the hatch from the movie Blast from the Past, with Christopher Walken, where he raises his son in a fallout shelter below the earth. It also makes him think of LOST, but only because the word hatch always reminds him of LOST. He is a big LOST fan, but that's because he's only seen the first two seasons and he never saw all that shit with time travel or the diamond thieves that get buried alive. He tries to pry the hatch open but it's closed tight. It won't budge. He doesn't try again because he's out in the open and so he walks back to the trees, and peeks back at the bar. That's when, I assume because I wasn't there and Sugar and I never discussed this, but this is when it would make sense for the girl—the assistant—to sneak out the back door. Which she did. Sugar watched as she gabbed away on her cinderblock sized cell phone, the old kinds like Zach Morris used to have, that looks like half a shoe box with a thick black antenna sticking out of the top. She is pacing briskly through the tall grass, annoyed and barking into the phone. Sugar Bear's curiosity is tickled and he walks towards her. He is surprisingly agile for someone with such a bulky size.

"This is unacceptable! We paid top dollar for the Tiger and now he's useless. You fucked us and this is not something that we will tolerate!" She bobbed her head angrily as she spoke on the phone. Sugar would later describe her to me in a way that made me picture her being a popsicle stick, like Stick Stickly from the old Nickelodeon channel. Bobbing up and down in space like a muppet. "No!" She screamed into the phone "My employer won't want to settle for an off the street replacement. We would want someone fresh off the line… yes….I don't care who it is, just grab someone and make sure they are ready in time!" Apparently she kept talking into the phone but this is when Sugar stopped listening to her and noticed something happening at the bar.

There was smoke, thick and grey, billowing out of the crack at the bottom of the door. And shouting, yelling and screaming coming from inside. I'm not sure how to describe the strange sound something makes when its body, which is mostly made of a milk-like substance, starts to boil and blister and bubble and curdle, but it's a terrible, horrendous noise. At least to Sugar Bear it's muffled by walls and boarded up windows. To me it's in my face, inside my head, and all around my body. Sugar Bear tilts his head, curious as to what could be happening, but also putting it together that there's a fire in the bar. Sugar Bear stands there, fishnet stockings and size 14 high heeled pumps, a leather thong, a baby blue sweater and a torn leather gimp mask—staring at the bar. This bar called the Grins & Smiles & Giggles & Laughs, burning down. Thick black smoke making swirling patterns in the sky, like heavy black rainclouds. Or the smoke monster from LOST. It's a nice picture, and would make for a beautiful still life painting. Sugar Bear notices a keypad on the side of the hatch. He bends down and starts to fiddle with it, he was an engineer after all, and he pops the back off the keypad to fuck with the wires. I guess disarming a keypad, or this particular one, is like crossing the wires of a car's engine to jump start it. So that's what he does and there's a loud click as the hatch unlocks. I'm not outside when any of this happens, so I'm assuming all of this. But I'm pretty sure I'm right.

He looks up and sees a figure making his way through the fire which is now stronger and bright blue as it takes over the building, painting the outside of the bar with bright flames. The figure is covered in a thick coating of protective, and apparently flame retardant bear semen. Sugar Bear smiles as he opens the hatch door.

"What the fuck happened in there?" He says to me.

"We need to find this lab," I say and look down at the open hatch. "What's that?"

"Only one way to find out." He says. And down the hatch we go.

It's a long way down but we reach the cold metal floor at the bottom. There's a deep, barely lit hallway that bends to the left. We hold still and listen to see if we can hear anything, but it's silent except for the hum of distant machines. We notice that there are wet spots and small piles of what look like slushy cereal swept up against the wall. But swept up like kicked against the wall, not neatly with a broom. The hallway does not lead us to the lab— not directly—instead it leads us to a room full of old mascot costumes. Giant costumes, as if there was once a plan for the mascots to just be people in outfits—big costumes that looked exactly like the cartoon mascots from the original boxes. I ask Sugar Bear about them but he just walks up to them and ignores me. He holds up the giant puppet-like head of Frankenberry, the big plastic eyes in the face have been etched out, as if scratched with keys or something. Sugar picks up another costume head, this one is of Tony the Tiger—his eyes are also scratched out. Sugar looks upset, as if he has seen these costumes before but is looking at them as if they should have been destroyed, like he's looking at ghosts of the costumes. "We have to get out of here."

"Why? What the hell is going on?" I am getting impatient and I'm still sticky and very uncomfortable.

"Lucky, listen to me. We have to get out of here."

"There's obviously something you're not telling me. Something to do with these costumes, I guess."

"I'm not sure what this means. But I don't like what this is making me think it *might* mean, so I'd rather not think about it."

He doesn't let me ask a follow-up question. He's already out the door and back into the hallway. I want to look around this room some more, thinking that I could figure out what Sugar Bear is hiding from me if I had more time to just take in the old costumes so more. But I realize how stupid that sounds the moment I think it. I'm not a detective, and the only reason I've gotten this far at all is because I've just been blindly following this bear around. So I go out into the hallway and continue to do just that.

The place looks more like the alleyway to an unlicensed abortionist than that of a sophisticated bio-lab. Again, I'm assuming as I've never been in an alleyway to an unlicensed abortionist or the hallway of a sophisticated bio-lab, for that matter. There's no reason to believe this tunnel leads to the lab, but I have a feeling. Why do we do that? Trust our feelings? I always found that expression strange, '*I have a feeling*' like, I think I know something I couldn't possibly know. I don't like that about myself. I don't like that I have gut feelings and follow them, that my instinct is to trust my instinct instead of learning from my mistakes and knowing that feelings don't mean a juicy jack shit when it comes to finding labs and getting facts. But, as it turns out, it seems like the gods of happy coincidences smile on us, because the feeling is right. We get to a row of windows and we see Soggies in white jumpsuits. They look like janitor scientists and they are all busy sloshing around this giant machine. It looks like one of those cartoon chemistry sets you'd see in shows like Dexter's Lab or that Halloween episode of the Simpsons where Mr. Burns has a lab and makes a giant metal robot with Homer's brain. I guess I could also have described it as giant beakers and conical tubes funneling into a giant Florence flask and cylinders labeled 'Condensed Mother's Milk' and 'Rice Bubbles'. They are pouring giant farm sized bags of rice krispies and buckets of milk into the cylinders. They are focused and have thick protective goggles on, and don't seem to notice a giant leather daddy bear and tiny semen soaked leprechaun sneaking through the hallway.

"What are they doing?" Sugar asks me.

"I'm not sure, but it ain't painting pancakes." I give him a wink. I'm very excited we've found the lab. I motion to Sugar Bear to follow me down the hall, he crouches down and tries to keep low.

There's a door at the end of the hall that leads to a room behind where the equipment is. We open it carefully and it makes a terribly slow and, at least to us, incredibly loud creaking sound. But nobody notices. We get the door open enough for Sugar to squeeze through, and walk into a large open room with arched ceilings that look like the inside of a whale skeleton. There isn't a good place to hide, except for a small corner of the room cast in shadow. The doors swing open and I jump behind the bear. We hold very still. We see two Soggies walk in followed by a cereal mascot. He's dressed in all red, and has a strong handlebar mustache that reminds me of Yosemite Sam. He has a long red scarf that trails behind him like a cartoon tail and has aviator goggles on top of his head, wearing them like a diadem. *Baron Von Redberry. The Baron.*

"That's him," I tell Sugar.

"That's who? Redberry? What about him?"

"Grapefellow was talking about the baron, how there is someone helping the Soggies take the mascots, I think this Redberry fuck is the guy!" We are whispering at each other, but I'm too excited to keep still. I try to get a closer look. Sugar grabs me by the shoulders and stops me.

"Shhh. We have to be careful." Sugar says.

"But it makes total sense that they would use a mascot to lure other mascots. This must be where they are taking them, but what are they doing to them?" An idea hits me. "We need to tackle him."

"Lucky, calm down."

"There's only two Soggies, you can take them out pretty quick. And all I need is a pool cue or something like that, and I can take care of the Baron. Jab that fucker in the dick."

"We still don't know what's going on. Let's just watch." He whispers.

I look at him from across the room, he seems dazed and drugged. Probably drunk. He doesn't seem like he would be much of a threat. The door next to us, the one we came through, opens and out comes one of those businessmen. He doesn't notice us in the shadows and walks right up to Redberry and they shake hands. Redberry seems standoffish, but he goes along with it.

I give Sugar Bear a 'See, why would the creepy businessman be making nice with Redberry if he wasn't involved in this?' look. He just shhh's me again and we keep watching.

I'm still not quite sure what this means, but this is when I become pretty sure that I'm getting close to cracking this whole thing open. That it has something to do with Redberry kidnapping mascots for businessmen who want to own a creepy sex slave. I am imagining the scene from the end of that Liam Neeson movie where his daughter is kidnapped and put into the world of sex trafficking. The movie is called Taken. I imagine that this is what I am going to walk into, and that—I let myself hope—Sam will be in one of these rooms. Drugged, abused but alive. I know that's not true, but in this moment, I believe it might be and it's the happiest moment of this story for me. These brief few seconds between seeing the businessman shake Redberry's hand and what happens next, are filled with this hope that somehow, and beyond all odds, things were going to be slightly better than I expected them to be.

But that's when this happens, the businessman licks his lips, and nods to the Soggies, they grab the dazed and what I assumed was drunk, but now I see might have been sedated, Baron Von Redberry and stumble-walk him towards the room with the giant lab equipment. They open the door and walk to one of the beakers. Sugar and I peek through the crack in the door, taking it all in. The businessman is standing outside the lab room, in the hallway, looking through the window. The beaker is filled with a thick white liquid that bubbles like molten hot gelatin. There is a ladder that leads to the mouth of the beaker. What happens next happens so fast that I can't react. Can't register shock or disgust, can't bring myself to spring into action and help, or run away to avoid the spectacle, so I take it all in. They push Redberry into the pile of marshmallow looking lava. It's terrifying how fast he sinks into it, how quickly he is liquefied, like a pile of warm butter. How red and thick the white substance gets. That's when the two cylinders filled with 'Condensed Mother's Milk' and 'Rice Bubbles' begin to pump into the beaker. Hot thick milk and a small hill's worth of Rice Krispie cereal get mixed into the bloody soup that was once the Redberry war pilot. The process doesn't take long.

Or maybe it does. I can't remember. All I know is that they are making what appears to be a giant, living, Rice Krispie treat out of Baron Von Redberry. They take the sludge from the beaker, once it's apparently mixed well enough, and pour it into a mold. There are still elements of the old mascot. You can still see the long red scarf, the aviator goggles, part of a red-tinted arm. The mold is large and square. They inject it, *him?*, not sure, with more of that condensed mother's milk and Sugar and I stare in shock at the strange glob of cereal that used to be a living breathing mascot, start to move. Small, sprout like legs and arms, pop out of its uneven, square frame. It has tine beady eyes that look like a monkfish's eyes. Or like the eyes of someone allergic to bees who has just been stung by bees. He moves forward, with difficulty, like Bambi taking his first steps. He looks up, confused and I can only assume frightened, and tried to make a sound with a tiny hole in his face that I'm realizing functions as a mouth. Two Soggies walk him towards a small door in the back and we see the businessman excitedly jog down the hallway and disappear behind a turn.

"We have to follow him," I say.

"No. We need to get the fuck out of here."

"I'm going to see what's going on. You should stay here, keep watch. Try to find a way out of here other than that stupid hatch. I'm sure they're looking for whoever burned down that bar by now."

Before Sugar Bear can say anything I take off down the hall. Full on leprechaun sprint.

I catch up to the businessman. He doesn't see me as he slows his jog and gets to a small ornate metal door. He seems a little nervous and excited, like he's about to meet a celebrity he likes at a Las Vegas meet and greet. It's more emotion than I've seen from any of these guys. He doesn't knock or anything, just waits at the door. Standing still, with his arms at his side. I'm impatient and I don't like that I have to wait for him to wait. I'm willing him to knock on the door or open it, but he just stands there like an excited kid at theater camp, waiting off stage for his entrance. I try not to let myself think too much about what I just saw, because if I do I might get sick and lose my nerve. But it's too late and I'm already re-playing the scene in my head. How fast and easy it was to turn someone into that creature. It reminds me of when my mother first taught me how to make Rice Krispie treats. I always assumed fancy baking was involved, that ovens and measuring cups and flour were part of the process. I was amazed at what I thought was culinary magic was simply heating up butter and marshmallows and adding cereal. It blew my fucking mind. It was its own kind of magic. I remember my mother would always eat them hot, not waiting for them to cool down and take the form of a square. She would serve herself a bowl of steaming hot Krispie treat oatmeal-like mush and smile like a five-year-old with an ice cream cone. I really miss her.

The door opens and I'm kicked back into the moment. A Soggie in one of those janitor lab coats opens the door and nods at the businessman. He walks in. I scurry along the floor and press my ear to the metal door, which isn't locked or even shut properly, and it eases open just a little. I notice that it's pretty dark inside and take a chance, walking in slowly and sticking to the darkness of the walls. There is a small dark purple lightbulb in the center of the room. Like a black light, and it illuminates a tiny circle in the center. The thing that used to be Baron Von Redberry wobbles into view. It looks up at the light bulb, almost hypnotized. I see the little businessman step into the light. He's naked and he is smiling ear to ear. I have a feeling I know what's going to happen, I have a feeling that this businessman is going to crawl on top of this living cereal treat and have sex with it. I think he's not only going to rape it, but he's going to eat it alive. He's going to rape this poor thing while he eats it to death. I don't know why I have this image in my head, but it's clear and it's horrible and I see it all flash in my imagination during the span of time it takes the businessman to walk into the light and hold the shivering square. I prepare myself mentally for it to happen, but it doesn't matter, I'm still very much not prepared at all for when my feeling turns out to be right.

The businessman is tearing into the krispietreat. He is thrusting into its warm marshmallowy body while biting into it. Blood and bone-jelly oozes from its body like a jelly donut, as it tries to scream with its tiny misshapen mouth. The business man is laughing through his mouthful, and I think he might choke, but he doesn't and carries on. Thrusting into the horrified and dying creature. Laughing and tearing at its fragile, cereal flesh, as he comes.

I am too shocked by all this that I don't notice the hairy paw on my shoulder turning me away from the snuff show I'm force-feeding my eyes.

"We got to get the fuck out of here." Sugar Bear is standing behind me. He looks really sad and tired. Like he also suspected something like this, and feels really horrible to be proven right.

"We have to leave. Now." He pulls me towards the door but I turn back and force myself to look at it some more. I just want to take as much in as possible, because this is what must have happened to Sam. And when I let myself think about this later, I want to torture myself with as much detail as possible.

We reach the woods outside. Sugar Bear found us an exit that takes us down the hill from the main lab entrance, by the old Raisin Bran Barn, where the Two Scoops rollercoaster used to be. We are very far away from the main park and Sugar Bear is throwing up in the bushes. Not sure why I connect those thoughts, because they are not related, but they are the two things I notice when we stop running. I'm not sure if Sugar Bear is vomiting because of what we saw back there, or because he just ran half a mile and is extremely out of shape and old. I believe it to be both.

I turn back to the direction of the lab, and realize that I have to go back, and that maybe—since we weren't being chased or anything like that—we didn't have to run so far away. I know that what we just saw pretty much confirms that Sam is dead. That what happened to Redberry happened to her. But that's not enough for me.

As if he was reading my thoughts Sugar Bear looks at me after wiping his mouth.

"Don't do it Lucky. She's gone. There's nothing you can do now."

"I have to go back, I have to make sure." I say, "And if something *did* happen to her I guess I need to do something about it. Like, I don't know, avenge her or something."

"You hardly spoke a word to her in years. You don't owe her anything."

"I owe her everything. You don't know our story. I'm really ashamed of a lot of things in that story. I fucked up and I owe it to her. I owe this to myself if nothing else."

"You're being ridiculous. We should leave. Right now."

I looked at Sugar Bear, knowing there was no point in trying to explain to him why this wasn't up for discussion. I've made up my mind, so convincing someone else that I'm not going to be convinced otherwise seemed like a waste of time.

"I'm going back." I say again. This time it's clear that I'm on a decidedly suicidal, self-serving mission and Sugar Bear just looks me over, taking in the fact that this is probably the last time he will see me alive, or at all. His look is sad and soft. It reminds me of the look my mother used to give me when I was a kid. I want to run over and hug Sugar Bear right now. I want to bury my tiny Leprechaun face into his giant bear rug of a body, and just cry. The kind of crying that makes it hard to breathe, and that forms snot bubbles on your face, and sounds like gasps and wailing. I want to cry for a long time, the kind that turns into maniacal and cathartic laughter and when I look up from his hairy body I want it all to have been a bad trip, that I got lost in daymare again and that when I come up for air I'm still just a marshmallow sorter and Sam is still just a cereal bartender. That we never went in for a mascot evaluation. That this never happened. But I'm not stupid, and I know that this is dumb of me to imagine, even for a tiny bit, because it makes me sad. It's heartbreaking to escape into a good fantasy because your shitty reality is that much worse when you come back to it. So I just look at Sugar Bear and keep my distance.

"You know Lucky," he says "It might not seem this way now, or even ever, but you truly are the luckiest guy I know. And I'm going to miss you."

I don't run over and hug him. I barely even make eye contact. I notice how fragile Sugar Bear is in this light, at this moment. He doesn't look like a giant bear anymore. He looks like a tired old man. He fishes out a pack of cigarettes and tosses it to me, along with a book of matches. I catch it and he winks at me. This makes me tear up, and so I turn and walk back towards the lab, without saying goodbye.

PART THREE

END OF THE RAINBOW

Lucky Charms Land was in the back of the park. It had a marshmallow garden where you could pick fresh mar bits off of trees and dip your hands into barrels of frosted lucky charm cereal. A small river of milk would flow through the trees and towards the giant Milk Fountain at the center of the park. The river would end up full of cereal that people would throw into it, making it a multicolored mush of soggy oats, corn and rice. The only cereal that would survive would be the Crunch Berries, little red and blue balls that would never get soggy and float across the thick river like the little heads of drowning children.

Toucan Tower, the Froot Loops section of the park, was on the other side of the property. Literally on the other side of the world, Cerealand-wise. It had rows of colored palm trees lining the entrance to the ride. Giant feathers provided shade on sunny days. And small animatronic toucans would sing and say hello, as you stood in line. The bright colors and funny birds a sharp contrast to the ride itself, which was a tribute to S&M and bondage. Toucan Sam, my Sam, was the star of her own burlesque show where she would be both dominant and submissive to other performers and people from the audience. This wasn't how the show always used to go. Apparently, the previous Sam was more of a traditional burlesque dancer—using her feathers like fans to cover herself up and tease the audience. Sam, my Sam, well—the Sam that used to be my Sam—she embraced this dark side I never really knew she was possible of embracing. When she became the Toucan, what I thought would be a way for us to reconnect, only alienated us more. She had been chosen as one of the top mascots, she had a new life, new friends, and lived in the main house with Tony the Tiger and Cornelius Rooster—while us lesser mascots had to live in dormitories. In fact, I don't think I ever had a real conversation with Sam since right before we both walked in for our mascot evaluations.

At first, things were great for her. Well, great is a relative term. But I guess in her mind, she was doing great. She was the star of her own show, and she seemed to love it. Selling out shows every night and being asked for VIP private window shows, because she could charge so much. At first, she would only do them occasionally. You didn't want to become a full-time Window Mascot. But every once in a while, for the right price, it was apparently worth it. I would hear all of this from Dig Em, who sometimes performed as her opening act. He'd open his huge frog gash of a mouth wide and let people throw anything they wanted inside it. It was demeaning and disgusting but the Frog seemed to be very proud of his show. But time isn't kind to most, especially for dancers, and it was harder and harder to keep her audience. Soon, the Toucan show began to lose its appeal. And Sam was forced to do more and more window shows.

So eventually she's in the window every night. Once you've become old news at the Burlesque show you have to be willing to do more and more things in the window for you to compete with the other acts. One of the more extreme things is when men in all black body suits and masks come into the room and use the mascot. It's like a live, barely permissive, rape show. After the mascot is used, the guys will sometimes piss on her or him, slap them around. In Sam's case they would yank at her feathers. Scratch and tug at her beak. You could turn on either scalding hot or freezing cold water for them to shower with afterward. It was a humiliation show.

So I save, I work and I don't (barely) smoke or curse. I take extra shifts and even sign up for Milk Duty. Earning enough, trying to earn enough, to buy us both out of our contracts. Pay for the surgery to turn us back to normal. But when I go to Sam and try to tell her what I'm doing she gets mad. She screams at me. She tells me to mind my own fucking business. And that she thinks it's creepy how I'm always trying to get involved in her life and run it for her. She tells me she's fine and she doesn't need my help. Which I guess is fair. It's her life after all and I wasn't in it anymore.

After that I stayed away for a while. But eventually my need to see her would win over any restraint I had. I would go to the pink windows. And would pay for the humiliation show. I would watch her try to give awkward blow jobs with her dumb toucan beak. Watch as she flinched with pain when they would slap her across the face or yank at her wing feathers. Watch as they beat her and pissed on her and left her staring at her broken and used reflection in the mirror. That might have been the most fucked up part of it, that you were forced to look at yourself, to watch yourself be used and broken. Knowing some sick fuck is just on the other side of the glass, smiling and getting off on your pain. The first time I saw her do it, I felt empty. I wanted to feel anger, or disgust. I wanted to feel empathy for her, or to break the one-way mirror down and save her. I wanted to feel love for her again. But I didn't. I just felt cold emptiness. The dullest and softest, but most consistent of pains. I wanted so badly to feel bad about what I was seeing. I didn't know why I put myself through that. I don't know why I would ever put *her* through that. But I did. I went back every night for a month. Every night I made her do it.

But I eventually stopped. It got a point where one night something happened. It took me over the edge, broke the protective veil I was using to keep myself from what I was doing, from really understanding what I was doing. And it was something so simple. As simple as her locking eyes with me. As if she knew.

There is no way she could know. The mirror was one-sided, it was tinted, plus a small mirror in the back of the window-room was there to let you see what the girl was seeing. A little reflection of her reflection was always dancing in the background. And yet it seemed like she was following my eyes, meeting my gaze no matter where I turned my head. I'd look at the corner and she's maneuver herself to that corner. Meet my eyes again. I knew she knew. I knew she could see me, and even if she couldn't—even if this was part my imagination and part incredible coincidence, she acted as if she could see me. See right through that glass as if it were a simple window. Normally she would cry, or show anger. She would sometimes even fight back, which in the end was all a part of the turn on for the customers, I assumed. It was for me, I guess. But the point is that she always had fight in her, always had a candle flicker behind her eyes. And that night, as she defied the laws of two-way mirrors and somehow saw through her reflection and into my eyes, that night when I looked into hers—I saw nothing. No light, no anger, no fear or shame, no fight at all. She just looked broken. And it broke me.

I broke eye contact with her, at that point, and I looked around. I stared at the other men and women widow shopping at the alley. Walking from pink lit window to pink lit window. I looked back at Sam, but I couldn't meet her eyes. I walked away and back towards my dorm. And I guess that was the last time I would ever see her.

I am thinking about Sam as I go back through the tunnel and into the lab. I am thinking about the way she used to argue with me about stupid things or how she would bore me sometimes, as I make my way past the hallway with windows, and the giant Dexter's Lab chem set that turns mascots into goop. I am thinking of all the times she infuriated me or upset me. The times she would lie. I am trying to get in the mindset to allow myself to bail if I sense things will get too difficult or scary. But I am full of shit. All I can really think about, beneath those thoughts, is how horrible Sam's life's last moments were. How furious and desperate I feel at knowing that she died terrified and eaten alive. And I know, as I charge ahead without a plan, that there is no way this ends well for me, but I will make it my mission to make sure it ends badly for everyone else as well.

I run into the large room, where I had hidden with Sugar Bear, and run to the door on the other side. It leads to a well-lit and carpeted room with two elevators. Instead of a button there is a keyhole. There's a couple of decorative bamboo in two floor vases next to the door, and an oil painting of Captain Crunch. I look for any other buttons or switches but there is no way to call for the elevator without a key. When I try to go back the way I came I see that the door has locked behind me and I'm trapped in this room. "You shouldn't be here Lucky." I hear someone behind me. I recognize the voice. That happy, optimistic voice. I turn around and one of the elevators is open, and Trix is leaning on the frame, keeping the automatic doors from closing. He's wearing the elevator key around his neck, like an asshole. Grabbing it in his hand and letting the key swing around like he's twirling a yo-yo. "You know," he says, once he realizes I'm just going to continue staring at him, "I had worked up this whole thing in my head, you know. Where I was going to come down here pretending I'd escaped. Tell you that Sam was alive, and was being kept in a holding cell somewhere in the lab, you know, something like that. I had this whole thing set up for you to really believe that you were going to be able to save her, and that I was going to be the one that helped you do it. I even had someone dress up in one of those toucan costumes we sell at the gift shop, so for a tiny moment you'd think you found her. And *that's* when I'd hit you with the big reveal that I double-crossed you." He was pacing in front of me now, the elevator door closing behind him. He had this proud smile, like he was enjoying describing this to me almost as much as he would have enjoyed actually carrying out his plan. "It would have been amazing," he continued "to see that moment. That priceless moment where you figured it out too late. But the Sisters said I couldn't do it. That we'd wasted enough time already. But they told me I could be the one to bring you in. You know, as a consolation."

I reached into my pocket and pulled out the cigarettes

Sugar Bear had given me, and the book of matches. I casually lit up a smoke and looked at the Rabbit.

"You're probably asking yourself, '*why?!, what did I ever do to you!?*' You were a terrible roommate Lucky! You are a horrible employee and you are an even worse mascot! You embarrass me and everything Cerealand stands for!"

He was pacing around excited now, you could tell he has been wanting to say this to me for a while.

"Look at you and your dumb idiot face," He said laughing "You don't get it, do you? Whatever it is you think you're doing, it doesn't matter. You've lost. It's all changing, Cerealand has to do drastic things if it's going to survive, to compete with what's out there. It has to appeal to a new world of people, a new class of clients. I had to help them! It was the only way to keep this place alive, it was the only way to keep this magical place going."

I smoke deep, it's keeping me centered and calm. I eye the bamboo in the vase closest to me, it's not exactly a pool cue, but it's close enough. I wait patiently for him to give me the perfect lead-in to a bamboo smack to the face.

"You're the baron?" I say. I guess it's a question, but I am pretty sure of the answer so I don't inflect the question mark.

"I don't really know where that nickname came from," says the Rabbit, "but it stuck. I've always liked it, made me sound like royalty, part of the Krispie family. It was either help them or become one of those *things*.

And Lucky, I love this place, but not enough to get made into living mush for it." He was smiling, distracting himself from the situation as he happily bragged to me. "Helping them bring in mascots for their new guests, that was the fun part. There are so many of you that don't deserve this gift! Don't deserve to be a Tony the Tiger or a Toucan Sam." He's not coming towards me, he's just standing there, looking very pleased with himself. I guess he's expecting more of a reaction from me. More shock or anger or disbelief. But I give him none of this. I'm just waiting, almost willing him, to say something about tricking me. I don't want to fish it out of him, because that feels like cheating, but I've got nothing left to lose on this kamikaze mission I'm on so I go for it.

"I guess you really fooled me. One could say you even..." I say, trying to give him a little of what he wants and nudge him in the direction of what I want.

"That's right you dumb shit, I got you good!"

That's close enough, and I grab a bamboo shoot and throw my whole body into the swing. I spin around like a helicopter, feeling the bamboo connect with the surprised Rabbit's face. I hear a satisfying sound combination of splintering bamboo wood and cracking rabbit cartilage, and Trix goes down, screaming as he holds in the blood gush that is coming from his face.

"Silly Rabbit. Tricks are for kids." I yank the key necklace off of him and call for the elevator. The doors open and I step inside.

"That would have worked a lot better if you'd said

'I *tricked* you good.' But you work with what you get."
I flick my cigarette at him as the doors closed.

Inside the elevator there were only two buttons. KL and OR. I assumed I was at the OR level, so I pushed KL and waited. The elevator didn't move right away, instead it rang, like I was calling an intercom. Someone picked up "Yes?"

I didn't say anything. I wasn't sure what to say.

"Yes?" The voice insisted.

"Um, delivery?" I said. I shouldn't have made that a question.

"Delivery of what?" The voice said. It seemed bored and agitated by this exchange.

"Delivery of justice," I said, and instantly regretted how lame that sounded out loud.

"What was that?"

"Nothing. A new Mascot. I'm delivering a new mascot."

There is a silence. Like they are checking something. I hear whispers like two people are discussing something urgently, quickly and in hushed tones.

"Come up." The voice says.

The elevator starts moving. I intended to use the ride up in the elevator to prepare a makeshift plan but then I realized I had left the bamboo shoot in the room with Trix. Fuck, I'm really not taking time to think here. I'm running in half-cocked and unarmed into a minefield and I'm not even taking the time to look where I step. I told myself, well a part of me told myself, that maybe I would die soon, and then I wouldn't have to think about any of this. Wouldn't that be nice? I wouldn't have to worry about getting out of here, or what the next move would be. I would die trying to set things right, and in the end that would be good enough for me. A noble death. But that's not going to be handed to me, I'm going to have to fight for it. A noble death doesn't count if you just roll over and let them kill you, it has to be earned. And you have to take down as much as you possibly can with you when you go.

The elevator stops. I hear a series of other locks outside the main door unlocking. Finally they open, slowly, like a curtain parting at an opera house, and there is Pop, smiling, sitting in a small chair with her hands neatly folded on her lap. She gives me a little hello nod and gets up.

"Follow me." She leads me towards a long hallway that fractures off into many different directions and sizes, from tiny hallways to giant and expansive ones. Her demeanor is cool and calm, which somehow makes me feel okay and regroup as I think my way into a plan. The hallways are strange and winding. I feel like I'm in a very boring deleted chapter of Alice in Wonderland. Do you remember how old cereal boxes would sometimes have little puzzles or games on the back of the box? Not a lot of people do, but my mother and I would always love solving those puzzles together. They weren't hard, the kind of stuff you'd find on a kid's paper placemats at a diner. Word jumbles, riddles, jokes. The best ones though, where the mazes. You would have to help someone, usually a cereal mascot, make their way through a series of turns in order to get to their prize, which was usually a bowl of cereal. But a few wrong turns and you'd face a dead end, or sometimes worse—actual death in the form of a monster or dangerous animal. Those mazes were always my favorite thing to do and one of the best things I used to associate with cereal and with my mom. As we walk down a series of twisting hallways, I imagine that we are in one of those cereal box mazes, and that all I have to do is avoid the alligators and minotaurs, and make it to the cereal at the end of the maze. The cereal in this case being swift and violent revenge on the psycho assholes who killed and ate my ex-girlfriend. That's the prize at the bottom of the box.

"We remember that day you asked us to reconsider your little friend. How you stood up to us. How you weren't afraid of us. That has always stood out to my sisters and me. It made an impression. We've overlooked small infractions of yours over the years, the smoking, the swearing, the way you go in and out of the Irish accent all the time. Things that would have cost a lesser mascot his or her job. But you've always been special. You get it Lucky. So many people don't get 'it'. The universal it. But you do. We *need* someone like that. Someone with vision—someone who can't help themselves from creating, from imagining, from leading."

"What the fuck are you talking about? Are you insane?"

"We've never seen things clearer. We know you are

different. You live in your head, you imagine, you create. You speak your mind. Just like papa. Now we weren't expecting you until later. I really hoped you would've taken my advice and stayed out of this. But it hardly matters now, right? You're here and you're going to be marvelous." She smiles at me.

"Not that you asked," I say to her "but I think eating all that mutated people meat has made you so brain-fucked batshit, that you can't think straight and you're taking a lot of liberties with your perception of me and your definition of reality. That's what I think."

She smiles, as if that kind of outburst is exactly the kind of thing she is talking about.

"You'll see." She says, insinuating she knows something about me that I don't know, which is insulting.

We get to the end of one of the hallways and see a row of doors. They are three revolving doors, and they have an almost fairytale, Goldilocks quality to them. One is small, slightly bigger than me. The other door is very thin and very tall. Like what a giant candy cane person might use. And the third one is very wide—and each section of the revolving door is the size of a small van.

I follow her through the smallest revolving door and we enter a giant ballroom. It's lit entirely by candlelight and it's very dim. There is a stage at the far end of the room with a crowd of people sitting in small plastic chairs facing the stage. Behind me and opposite the stage, is a large expansive balcony with three chairs that mirror the dimensions of the revolving doors. All of this is very curious, but I'm still very mad and try keeping my cool long enough to figure out what is going on and how I'm going to be able to strike when the Achilles heel of this place reveals itself to me. The chairs are full of people wearing masks. I recognize that they are the businessmen from before by their suits, their shiny shoes. But they are wearing plastic masks of different cereal mascots. I stare at someone wearing a Lucky the Leprechaun mask, its eye holes vacantly staring at me, and it's strangely comforting. Pop is leading me down the row of chairs towards the stage. I'm so distracted scanning the room and looking at all the businessmen in masks that I completely ignore the fact that there is something on stage. Someone sitting in a tall golden throne, well it looks golden, it could be gold plated. It's tall and impractical, like a cross between a fancy high chair and lifeguard's perch. And there, sitting on it, in a faded navy blue officer's uniform, worn down copper buttons lining its outer coat, barely protected by a blood and marshmallow stained bib, is what has to be a barely alive, Captain Horatio Crunch.

He looks, and I'm guessing here, 100 years old. A dribble of thick old man drool connecting his chin to his bib.

I can't believe it. It's hard to describe how something can be so pathetic and so terrifying at the same time. His eyes were cloudy, like that of an old sick dog, milky and half-blind. His liver-spotted skin clung loosely to him as if his whole body was the loose skin on an old person's neck. Like every part of him was made out of a turkey's waddle. His thin white mustache, like the bristles of an old used toothbrush, hung over thin blood stained lips and teeth, that looked like he'd been eating nothing but beets for years. He reminds me of the old man in Texas Chainsaw Massacre. Grandpa Sawyer. The patriarch of the family that is drooling all over himself and that still somehow controls this family of incredibly dangerous, inbred cannibals. I guess this here is a lot like that, what with them eating and killing people. At least the family in Texas Chainsaw didn't rape and eat their victims alive. They had the decency to slaughter them and then cook them once they were dead. That movie, to many people, is considered the definitive or at least the modern reinvention of the horror film. It pretended to be based on real events and that made people think stuff like this was normal enough that a Hollywood movie could be made about it. I know that horrible things that people do to each other have been around for a lot longer than the movie The Texas Chainsaw Massacre, but I also believe that there would be a lot less creepy old men eating people they have their family kill, if they didn't have a movie they could connect with and point to, a film that inspires and justifies their situation. He is also very small. Like smaller than me. He looks like a very young child pretending to be a very old man.

Captain Crunch, or what cognitive part of him was left, looked down at me with his half blind eyes. Then he looked at Pop and lifted his brittle arm, pointing his index finger towards his mouth. The crowd applauded this basic movement from him as if he had just composed a symphony or juggled eight glass eggs. Pop clapped excitedly—"Oh goody, it's snack time." She smiled at me, "My sisters should be here any moment."

The crowd turned their heads towards the giant balcony behind us, and the purple velvet curtain opened up to reveal Crackle and Snap. I had only ever seen them in shadow, and this was years ago, and they never really made an appearance at the park so this was a significant moment. At most they would sometimes introduce the parade, but that would normally only be through the park's announcement system. This was my first real look at Pop's older sisters, and they are a lot more grotesque and different from Pop than I could have ever let myself imagine. What I am looking at stops me cold. Any semblance of a plan or drive to attack is quelled as I take in these monsters. Before I go into trying my best to describe them to you, I should set the context a little better, and again, this is all assumption, but I figure that there must be women who own or have married into owning their own plastic surgery practice, and that even though at first it may start off small, a tummy tuck here, an injection of botulinum toxin there, soon, like I imagine tattoos to be, it becomes an addiction. There is always room to improve, to become better, tighter, smaller, bigger. Similarly I think that if you owned a machine that changed you on a genetic level, and could make you a monster, a powerful and scary creature, then—at least if you were these two owners of a cereal and sex-themed amusement park, then I guess you go all in.

Seeing them all together, I realize that Pop is the most normal one. I use normal very loosely here, because she still looks like some kind of rejected Manga character. But when she's next to Crackle and Snap, she looks as almost pedestrian and boring. Snap is tall, impossibly so, wiry and thin as if she were made of old dry branches and twisted up copper wire. Like Pop, the only thing that points to the fact that she's supposed to be a cereal mascot is the tiny white chef's hat on her strangely shaped head and red kerchief tightly tied around her branch-like throat. She must stand at least 14 feet tall, and looks like what Jack Skelington must have looked to the kids in a Nightmare Before Christmas. But instead of a happy skeleton face, Snap has a face that looks like an old raisin. It is all wrinkled and it's hard to tell where her eyes, nose and mouth are or if she even had any. I know very little about Slenderman beyond the fact that many many years ago some kids stabbed another child a whole bunch of times because Slenderman told them to do it. The few images I've come across of him, make him look tall and thin and faceless. Snap looks like something Slenderman would be afraid of. Snap looks like the truly abusive mother, Bates motel level of abuse, to Slenderman's Norman Bates. She steps off the high balcony and onto the floor, her thin and thorny legs landing close to me as she makes her way towards the throne.

Snap approached her father, who continued to look down at me, yellow spittle waterfalling from his gross old mouth. Snap removed his hat and gave him a soft kiss on the forehead. I guess she does have a mouth. She turned and looked at Pop who nodded and signaled to a Soggie who nodded back. The Soggie walks behind a small curtain, and comes back leading one of the Mascot Treats by the hand toward Pop. The Mascot Treat looks scarred and confused, like Redberry did. I can't really tell who that used to be, but I see parts of aprons and a chef hat, half a pair of eye glasses, and I figure it must be one of the Cinnamon Toast Crunch chefs. There are cinnamon swirls, like birthmarks, all over the Treat, so I am pretty sure I'm right, but it doesn't really matter at this point.

Pop walks to the front of the stage, at the foot of her father's high chair, and addresses the small crowd. "Family. Here at Cerealand we are a family. And tonight, although slightly ahead of schedule, we honor our father." The businessmen in masks nod and murmur in excited approval.

"For he will not be with us much longer, but his spirit and his ideals will endure through his children." The crowd agrees, cheering and chanting. "We are blessed by his love and his guidance, his vision grants us freedom and power."

"Freedom and power." The crowd repeats. It has the back and forth cadence of a church or a kindergarten.

I scan the room, making an inventory of anything I can use as a weapon, keeping in mind that I am too small to pick up most things. Maybe I can kick out one of the legs of his stupid throne, or tip him over. I wonder if I could do that before his freak daughters saved him. Probably not.

"Cerealand is a special place," Pop is now taking the Treat mascot by the hand, leading it to Snap who crouches down to pick it up. "It's a place where special things happen for special people." She's looking at me now, directly at me. "And we need someone to help steer this ship as it were. Keep us on course. Navigate the storms to come."

I don't know where to look so I just meet her gaze and hold it.

"Tomorrow, a new dawn will rise and we will set sail towards new horizons, with new hands to steady the wheel." She smiles at me and then goes back to addressing the crowd. "Tonight," she adds, "We eat!"

Snap, living up to her name, splits the living Treat in half. Muffled sounds of agony fill the room along with the oddly satisfying sound of wet gooey entrails and bone jelly thwacking against a cold stone floor. The businessmen cheer and jump out of their chairs, holding their hands behind their backs, like you would in a pie eating contest, they attack the wet gobs on the floor, slurping the treat through the tiny slits in their masks. The slurping is almost worse than the screaming. No, not almost—it is worse. Snap is feeding bits of bloody cinnamon treat to Captain Crunch, who mushes the food around with his teeth before swallowing half of it and letting half fall out of his useless old mouth. It's like watching someone feed a harlequin baby an old raw hamburger covered in sugar. I have to turn away and that's when I look over at the balcony. I've been so distracted by Snap and the speech Pop was giving that I didn't give much thought to Crackle. But when I turn to take her in, it takes me a while to understand that everything I'm seeing is all one person. Every time I think I've gotten to the outline of her body, I find that there's more. She's enormous. Crackle is sitting in a gigantic bean bag chair, or it's more like a huge Papasan, but I mean it's the size of a small swimming pool. She reaches over to a bucket filled with piles of wet cereal. She grabs a handful and slowly eats at it. Nibbling at the soggy oats in her hand like a gerbil. I can't get over how huge she is. I mean I know she must seem huge to someone little, but she is objectively the biggest thing I've ever seen. Huge in the sense that I am not sure how that balcony is holding her up there. How she is not collapsing into herself like a dying star. It's hard to describe her. Maybe you've seen the movie What's Eating Gilbert Grape. It's a movie with Juliette Lewis and in it there's this character, Gilbert Grape's mom, played by Darlene Cates, who is so big that when she dies, her kids burn the house down with her in it because there is no way to get her out of the house without it becoming a spectacle. She won't fit through the doors. If you haven't seen the movie, there's also an episode of the show American Dad where they play out that part of the movie using squirrels that live in Steve's treehouse, and you've probably seen that. Point is that in this movie and episode of American Dad, the mom is so big that she can't leave the house, well Crackle is like that, but more—much more. Like if ten of those moms merged together and made Jabba the Hutt look like a toy poodle, then you can come close to imagining the impressive and intimidating force of nature that was Crackle, perched on the balcony, softly nibbling at her fistful of wet Cheerios. She looked almost disinterested in the…ceremony, I guess I'll call it, not at all paying attention to what her sisters were doing. Keeping her eyes on the prize—her bucket of cereal mush. I'm not sure what's more unsettling, seeing Snap feed the old Captain as he half ate his bloody meal, or watching Crackle slurp up tiny bits of wet cereal like a bird making out with its food. I felt sick. I decided Crackle wasn't much of a threat so I turned my attention to the old doddering freak in the high chair above me. He was finishing up the bit of food that Snap had placed in his open mouth. Snap used his bib to clean up his face and stroked his cheek with the back of her dry, splintery hand. Pop saw me staring at her father. I think she mistook this for wonder or reverence instead of awestruck disgust, because she smiled at me and looked over to Crackle. Crackle, still busy gingerly licking the cereal pulp from between her fingers, didn't look back. Pop rolled her eyes and tapped Snap on the ankle. Snap bent her long, spidery body down to Pop.

"I think it's time they met." Said Pop. Snap turned back to Crackle, who again was too busy with her cereal slush to pay them much attention. Snap cocked her head, as if to ask Pop if she was sure.

"Stop treating me like I don't know what I'm doing!" Whined Pop. "I think it's time. Right Lucky?"

She looked at me. For some reason I remembered, at that moment, the fact that she had breastfed me when I first turned into Lucky. A thought that made me laugh a little at the absurdity of it all, and the strange and stupid journey that had gotten me here. It must have read as nervous excitement instead of what it was, which was the laugh of someone who has nothing left to lose.

There's a memory I used to go to a lot, especially when I first started working at Cerealand. My mother and I used to eat cereal together on Sunday nights. We would sit on the bed in her room, and place a beach towel over the sheets in case we spilled milk. She loved the show "America's Funniest Home Videos" and every Sunday she would download an episode and we would watch it together with a bowl of cereal resting on our laps. If you've never seen that show, it's basically people getting hurt while a comedian does silly voices over the footage. My mom thought it was the best show ever made. I think she liked it because it showed that people could get over their shame and embarrassment and become proud of their dumb mistakes. Even if it was all so they could win a prize.

My dad would always be working on Sundays, and

SIMON ORÉ MOLINA

so it became a tradition that she and I would do. Her favorite cereal was Apple Jacks, and her favorite thing to do while she ate them was tell me how much she hated the Apple Jack commercials. She complained that they made no sense and they infuriated her with how stupid they were—how they didn't even have a cartoon mascot for the cereal. That's what really got her. She would say that she always wanted to work at a cereal company, help them design cartoon mascots. I think my mom secretly enjoyed hating things as much as she enjoyed loving things.

One day, and this is the specific memory I go to, mom taught me how to make Rice Krispie treats. I had seen them before, in vintage commercials and on old tv shows—they were this magical, marshmallowy square that held all the cereal together in a buttery hug. I was sure that you had to be a skilled and learned baker to make such a thing. My mom told me she was teaching me to make them, and I laughed at her, told her we didn't even own a stove. She smiled and grabbed a mixing bowl and put in a few sticks of butter, a bag of marshmallows and a box of rice krispie cereal. Then she popped it into the microwave and plugged in about 8 minutes. She looked at me, smirking, and told me they'd be ready in a sec. I was floored by this. I couldn't fucking handle it. Something so magical was so easy and practical to make?! That shit didn't make sense to me. I didn't know if I was thrilled at how simple it was or horribly saddened by how mundane everything I thought was magical ended up becoming. My mom grabbed the mixing bowl out of the microwave and set it on the table. She looked up at me and gave me a sad smile. "Do me a favor kiddo, don't ever live your life for someone else. You got to live your life for you." I'm not sure why she said that, even now it seems so out of character. And I know I should have asked what she meant, taken this moment to get to know my mom, but I felt uncomfortable and I just wanted to eat our cereal and watch America's Funniest Home videos like we did every Sunday. So I didn't ask her and she didn't say anything else. Every time I think about this day I wonder why she said what she said and what she was trying to say by saying it. But I still don't really know. And I never asked her about it before she died.

We ate the treats hot, right out of the bowl, with big wooden spoons.

Snap stared at me with that wrinkled mess of a face and picked me up in her long twig arms. I smiled, looking excited, since I realized that's what they wanted from me. She lifted me up in the air and displayed me to the room, Lion King style, and the hungry businessmen below looked up from their floor meals only to bow their heads down in respect. Snap shakes me a little, using me to get Crackle's attention, who looks up at Snap and I and then at Pop. She makes a strange and very subtle expression—almost as if conveying 'If that's what you want to do, go ahead.' But in a very condescending way. Snap looks to Pop and Pop nods, an 'it's good—we're good' kind of nod.

Snap turns me and places me on the lap of the old man. Up close he is even more decrepit and nasty looking. Stains and smells of all kinds of colors are all over his tiny blue pants and his captain's coat. His hands are doing that old person shake, you know, where they can't help but be shaking in that unsettling way that makes you feel bad for them but also makes you feel like they are contagious and that you should not let them touch you. His hands are shaking like that. Up close I see that his eyes are totally milked over and his body, his actual skin, is made of Captain Crunch cereal. It's brittle and a lot of it has cracks in it. His face is old and droopy, but still hard and crispy?—is crispy the word I'm looking for? What I thought were liver spots are actually crunch berries baked into his skin, and up close they look like cancerous polyps.

The crowd is staring at us. The room is dead silent. It's like they are watching a magical moment for them. I look out into the ballroom and watch Pop, who is smiling, beaming, at me. Almost proud. I look at Snap, her faceless raisin head cocked to the side, like a cute curious dinosaur. And then I look at Crackle, who raises her head towards mine and gives me the faintest of smiles. And then finally I look at the Captain. I look right in his gross milky eyes and I know he sees me. He moves his shaky old hand towards me, as if to hold me tighter or maybe shake my hand, I don't know.

I want to tell you that when I look into his eyes I

see a pathetic old man who I pity, or even better, that I see pure evil, that even though he is an old useless shit of a man, that I see the fire in there that created and forged this hell and I will be able to take him down, and have him know he has been beaten. I wish I could tell you that in this moment everyone I've lost flashes before my eyes and the anger inside me is finally unleashed. That I hulk out and despite being a tiny leprechaun, I muster the courage to do what I do out of defiance and purpose. But that's not the case. The truth is I look into his eyes and I see nothing. Nothing but an empty, slightly mad, milky white stare. It makes me feel empty. Still, I'm here. I made it here, and I'm not going to just sit around with my thumb up my ass. I get an idea. I smile because the idea is so smart and simple and yet it's the kind of idea that could only come to me in the moment. I look toward the crowd of Business Men and Women in masks below me and I look right at Pop, who beams at me, as if willing me to say it, almost mouthing the words. "Part of a Complete Breakfast!" I shout. The crowd cheers and chants back "Part of a Complete Breakfast!" I smile widely at the old man and I know he sees me, because he gives me what can arguably pass as an approving nod and smiles back. And I'm not sure if he's mirroring me, or if he genuinely thinks he knows what's going on, but that doesn't matter to me as I bite into his crunchy flesh, tearing at his throat with my tiny leprechaun teeth. Although his skin is made of captain crunch cereal, his insides are still human and I almost gag when my mouth fills with thick blood. The blood is sweet though, and tastes like birthday cake flavored maple syrup and dirty pennies. But I can't stop to gag or comment on it, I keep biting, deeper and deeper until I am hitting bone. This has to happen in a few seconds, tops—because it doesn't take long for Snap to pull me off her father's lap and toss me across the room.

Snap is cradling her father in her long, coat hanger arms. The tiny misshapen mouth in the middle of her prune face is wailing. She is pressing her hands against the wounds, trying to keep the blood from oozing out—but it's too late. He's gone. She holds him close and shrieks. She hugs his little body to hers and breaks down, curling up into a ball in the corner, cradling Captain Crunch's body and sucking on his wound. Crying softly and she licks him clean. Her long scratchy tongue eeks out of her mouth like a slimy tree branch, and like a mosquito's proboscis, starts to drink him dry. She is making soft whimpering noises.

I get up slowly, my whole body aches and I think my ankle is sprained. I can't put any weight on it. Pop is walking towards me. Her face is a twisted pretzel of rage and disappointment. Even if I die right now, I think, and there's a pretty solid chance that I will die right now, this moment, this moment of having crushed the Krispies and taken something from them, something important, was worth it all. Well, worth most of it.

Pop walks to where I'm slowly getting up. She shows no emotion on her face, no anger, no sadness—which I think is downright terrifying, given the circumstances. I am waiting for her to strike at me or say something, but she just stands there. Looking at me. Slowly taking in my every detail. I can tell she is playing chess, she is mapping out her moves and figuring out when the death blow is going to be, but she's in for some shitballs luck, because I'm doing the same thing. I am seeing the map of our fight spread in front of me and I know that as long as they fight fare and I fight dirty, I will have a chance of getting out of here. But before I can say this to myself in a way that sounds convincing and gets me excited about the idea, Pop punches me in the throat, right in the Adam's apple, and I go down, gasping for breath. I get up fast, knowing that if I let her get the best of me right away there will be no coming back. I am still struggling to breathe, but I think that if I can get to slightly higher ground, like the stage, I'll be able to get the upper hand, and as I think this Pop grabs a plastic chair and swings it at my head. I fly backwards like a nerf dart and land in the circle of businessmen eating. They clear the circle and surround me on all sides. They chant. "eat. eat. eat. eat. eat." They are acting like cavemen and I wonder what kind of businesses would employ these assholes.

Pop jumps into the circle and smiles. These are her people, her turf, her father's death fueling her. This seems like the perfect recipe for Pop to succeed, but you forget one thing, I am also fueled by love and revenge, and I've had time to distill this feeling and make it so pure and strong that it is stronger than anyone else's need to love or avenge. I take a swing at Pop, who ducks it easily and then bashes me with another chair. This time I get knocked to the floor and it leaves me dazed and dizzy. Pop takes out a small riding crop, like the kind you use to whip a horse into going faster. She walks up to me, and before I can rush at her, tackling her to the ground, my plan is foiled by her hitting me across the face with the riding crop. I look at her and notice she is teary-eyed, but stoic, however her eyes are shining with sadness and excitement. By the look on her face this seems like a very cathartic moment for her. The circle of businessmen are cheering us on as we pace around each other. Pop seems unscathed, even emotionally she is keeping it together. She looks at me as we circle each other like suspicious sharks. But she has a calm about her. Like her father's death was an inevitability, but she just wasn't expecting it to happen like it did.

"Why are you doing this?" I ask

"Why do anything."

"Well that's not a helpful way to answer a question."

"You made a very big mistake, Lucky. But it's nothing we can't fix." She keeps walking around the circle, and I am mirroring her, head spinning and ankle throbbing, but still in what can sort of pass as an attack stance.

"You're the right dimensions for the costume" she continues, "and we still have his DNA. Sure, it will be mixed with a little bit of leprechaun but we can make sure that you are as close to the original as possible. Doesn't that sound fun Lucky? Being the Captain? Controlling the park, the rides, the mascots, all of it!"

I tried to push my way out of the circle, but the businessmen just pushed me back in, and got closer together, tightening the gaps in between their bodies so I couldn't sneak through.

"There's no use fighting it Lucky. It's going to happen regardless of how you feel, you might as well be open to accepting it."

I stop moving and so does she. I didn't realize I was leading this dance. I am pretty beat up and tired, I just want this to end. Pop can read this on my face. She gets closer to me, dropping the riding crop. She reaches out to comfort me, and I let her. She holds me in her arms and hugs me. And that's when I make my move—with a swift, strong uppercut to her stupid face. I connect hard, it hurts my hand because I'm stupid and leave my thumb inside my clenched fist, which I've heard you're not supposed to do. Pop stumbles back, genuinely shocked. I take off one of my shoes and start hitting her with it, furiously beating the shoe against her chest and arms as she tries to fend me off. The business men keep cheering, they don't seem to care who is winning as long as there is a fight. And as far as I can tell Snap is still in the corner licking up her father's blood. I keep striking down on Pop as hard as I can. I'm going after her nose now, but instead of covering her face, she takes the blow full on, but doing so lets her reach down and grab my left leg. She pulls on it and I stumble backwards. She stands up and looks down at me, blood pooling in her shirt from her fractured nose. She isn't smiling anymore and her purple dot eyes narrow. Pop comes at me and it's shocking, she moves with the grace of an ice skater and the intense fury of a charging rhino. It takes me a second to realize that I've been knocked down again and that she is on top of me, pinning my arms to my sides. She takes a deep breath and raises her arms, her hands making a kind of sledgehammer fist where both her hands are clenched together. I look at up her, she's getting ready to come down on me with everything she's got, and in that moment I see the desperation in her face, and I wonder what it was like for these girls growing up. How I'm sure now that it must have been their father, directly or not, that made them do this to themselves. To turn themselves into these horrible deformed versions of themselves and host these fucked up snuff orgies. I could see Pop was so tired, and so over this life, even if she didn't see it herself—it was a second, a tiny half moment, but I saw it. And I felt sorry for her. For all of them.

I closed my eyes and waited for Pop to lower her fists down onto my face when I heard this booming voice—like an echo that speaks first, but coming from inside my own head. Though it's clear from the reaction of the crowd that everyone heard it.

ENOUGH. It said.

The whole room, Pop included, turned away from me and looked up at the balcony. Crackle was looking out at us. The room went still. Pop got off me and walked over to the stairs that lead her up to her sister. There was a respectful and hush tone in the room, and I realized that Crackle must be the eldest sister, the one in charge. Which makes her distracted eating more of a power move than a hedonistic glutton move, now that I think back on it. I'm slowly getting up off the ground to get a better look at what's happening in the balcony. No one is looking at me, and I think back on this moment as the moment I might have been able to run away, but I don't. I'm just as interested in what's going on as everyone else.

Pop and Crackle are having a silent exchange, and I try to figure out what it is based on facial expressions and body language. I get a lot from Pop who seems to be wordlessly saying things like 'he killed our father' 'he must be punished for it' 'i don't care what you think!' And 'I guess you're right but I'm not happy about it.' And finally 'you're right. It will never be the right time. And I'm sorry I yelled at you. I Love you."

When I look at Crackle, she gives off nothing but a sharp, focused gaze and a labored chewing.

Crackle grunts and Pop backs away, subservient. She grunts again and two Soggies come into the circle of businessmen and help me to my feet. They walk me up the stairs onto the second floor and place me in front of Crackle. She and I lock eyes and she gives me a look.

It's a kind and sympathetic look. It's an understanding look. But it's also a stern look. It's the look of a tough but fair teacher or a no-nonsense grandmother. And it's like I can hear a voice in my head, her voice, and it's quite soft and soothing. It's a beautiful and calming voice and I listen to it. I just let it talk to me.

The voice somehow conveys to me that yes, it knows that this is terrible and yes I am right to be confused, to be shocked and full of justified anger. The voice also tells me, calmly and lovingly, that there is simply nothing I can do. I am too small. I am too weak. I can't really do anything that will stop what is happened, or reverse what has already happened.

But I have a chance to change that. A choice to make. To change the course of the rest of my story. To embrace it!

Her eyes are shiny, like anime eyes, and they don't blink. And the voice is making a lot of sense. But I resist this, I try to shake this off and say to myself and this monstrous thing in front of me, that I would rather die than go along with what they are doing. That I'd rather burn with them than just allow them to have gotten away with it. I think at her that I still have fight in me. That I am good and they are bad and that good is supposed to somehow get an advantage in moments like these. That Sugar Bear is going to crash into the room, any second now, with all the surviving mascots, and help me take these bitches down!

But none of this is true. None of this seems convincing to me or to her. And as I stare at her, I know she's right. I know that I am out of options. I feel cheated. I feel like I am owed a confrontation, that I was robbed of my final moment of battle that I was having with Pop—that fight felt more honest than this flaccid surrender.

I make one last pathetic attempt to do right by Sam, I say her name out loud. As if that in itself is a question or an accusation. Just her name. Samantha. As if reminding myself, and the room, why I started this. As if saying her name would make them realize that there is no reasoning with me and that I am here to watch this all get destroyed. But I have to admit to myself that I am not ready or willing to die. It sounds like a romantic thing to believe in, willingly dying for a cause, for someone you love, or used to love, but it's actually very hard to do. And I let myself feel disgust, and I let myself admit that I've failed, that I didn't do enough to save her.

I don't have to say anything. Crackle doesn't have to say anything. I just lower my head in shame and submission.

Snap, having licked the captain clean, steps out of the corner and comes towards us. She leans over and picks me up, like a mother picking up a tired toddler, walks me across the ballroom and places me on the tall, ornate throne.

Her hands are scratchy, like branches made of sandpaper and I don't even feel it when she places the blue shipmaster hat on my head. The Soggies line up at attention, even the businessmen and women in masks are bowing their heads slightly at me. The sisters smile and hold hands. "Long Live the Captain!" They say. "Long Live the Captain!" The room echoes back. I'm too weak and defeated at this point to do anything but let them chant. I still have the taste of the old captain in my mouth, and I move my tongue around in my mouth, smiling.

I look down at the crowd from the high chair throne and they all look so small to me. Like little candy people. It's been a long time since I felt taller than anyone, bigger and stronger than anyone. It's like I could scoop them all up and place them in a giant blender, get rid of them all and start fresh. Make this place fun again. Turn it into something wonderful.

I look at the room full of people in cereal mascot masks, and I lick my lips.

I was talking to Sam as she was cleaning up the cereal bar after closing. I had spent all day sorting Marshmallows and Sam had spent all day dealing with drunks and serving them whisky soaked Cocoa Puff shots and Cinnamon Toast Sangria. I was looking over the Cerealand Mascot Application forms.

"There's a lot of stuff we have to agree to and sign off on before we can even be considered. There's a morality clause, we would have to be in character 24/7" She was only half listening to me. She didn't seem to care about any of the logistics and the risks, she just wanted to do it.

"But you're right, the pay is amazing. And they do say that they can change you back once your contract expires." This was good news, but she turned and frowned.

"What if I don't want to change back?" she said

"What do you mean?"

"I mean," she said, annoyed that I wasn't getting it immediately, "what if I want to stay a Cereal Mascot?"

"Why the fuck would you want to do that?"

She didn't answer me, she just looked at me like I was stupid. I loved it when she looked at me like that. She took the application from me and grabbed a pen. "Well, I'm going to do it." She said and began filling out the application.

"But I haven't even read it all, you don't know what you're agreeing to. And the little

I've understood from what I did read, it really looks like this is a bad deal. I don't think we should do it." But I was speaking to deaf ears, this one had made up her mind a long time ago and was going to do it with or without me. She signed the last page and then handed me the pen and the other application.

"So, you coming with?" she said with her sly smile and crinkled nose. Of course I was. I'd follow that nose anywhere.

ABOUT THE AUTHOR

Simon Oré Molina is an imaginary friend for hire and a lover of snacks, especially chips and cereal. In addition to watching cartoons, smoking on the porch, whittling flamingos, and listening to *They Might Be Giants* music, he is head of development at the animation studio Starburns Industries and is the founder of SBI Press, the imprint of Starburns that makes Comic Books, Art Books and Limited Edition Cassette Tapes. His love of cereal is well documented as he is the co-host of an all you can eat cereal bar and Saturday Morning Cartoon showcase at the Bob Baker Marionette Theater in Los Angeles, CA. Simon is also a founding member of El Cine—a nonprofit organization that promotes diversity in film and has screenings of LatinX films with their creators.

Originally from Montreal, Canada, Simon moved to Acapulco, Mexico, and now lives in Los Angeles, California where he is left handed.

ACKNOWLEDGEMENTS

No one reads this part of the book, unless you know the author personally and are checking to see if they included your name. So it's really only here to placate narcissism. I have lots of people I can thank for helping me with this book specifically, good friends and family members who gave me notes and guidance, my editor and everyone at Eraserhead Press and the Bizarro Community at large—and I could also easily thank those who have helped me in life in a general sense, who always encouraged me or believed in me and supported me. My family is incredible, I'm lucky to have them and I love them more than sugar, but they already know this. And so do my friends.

So instead I will use this moment to write about something more important. Colony Collapse Disorder. It's this disease that is killing off all the bees! If the bees die, then so much of the food we depend on will die—and there will be no more honey. Do you understand this? No. More. Honey. Ever. (And don't start with your Maple Syrup horseshit). I guess it's important to state that I'm talking specifically about honeybees and not bumble bees or wasps or hornets of any other useless species of comparable insect—I am talking about the honeybees.

A lot of people know this, but some may not, and that's

that bee's do NOT want to sting you. They die when they sting you. It's a goddamn last resort when they think you are a danger or threat to them and their hive. They would leave you the fuck alone if you didn't start screaming and waving your arms around like a maniac and looking like a goddamn monster from the Cloverfield movie. Bees are essential to our ecosystem—not just THEIR ecosystem, OUR ecosystem.

I remember when I was a kid, throwing rocks at an underground beehive that was buried within a hill near my house in Montreal. My friends and I had gathered around this hill that had a hole in it and dozens of bees were coming in and out of that hole. It was an incredible thing really, to see them build a Hobbit hole in the middle of this hill. Defying everything I knew about hives. But we were terrible little pieces of shit and we saw the bees as enemies—we threw rocks at their hive and I (in a turn of justice for the bees) got stung. The pain was intense, and I thought I was going to lose my arm. I was sure the only cure was to just severe the arm entirely. But no, I healed. And that bee that stung me, protecting its home, most likely died from it.

I don't have a solution here, I don't know what can be done to help the bees. I guess you could all start keeping beehives, and I guess I should start that trend myself instead of just talking about it. If I had my own hive, I could care for those bees, keep them safe and plant lots of flowers for them to have sex with, and I could harvest fresh honey regularly, and I could use that honey to sweeten my cereal. Thank you, Bees.